Random Reflections of a Looney Bin

Random Reflections of a Looney Bin

Gordon Kerkham, RN, RNMS, RPN, MNP

iUniverse LLC
Bloomington

RANDOM REFLECTIONS OF A LOONEY BIN

Copyright © 2013 Gordon Kerkham, RN, RNMS, RPN, MNP.

All rights reserved. No part of this book may be used or reproduced by any means, graphic, electronic, or mechanical, including photocopying, recording, taping or by any information storage retrieval system without the written permission of the publisher except in the case of brief quotations embodied in critical articles and reviews.

iUniverse books may be ordered through booksellers or by contacting:

iUniverse LLC
1663 Liberty Drive
Bloomington, IN 47403
www.iuniverse.com
1-800-Authors (1-800-288-4677)

Because of the dynamic nature of the Internet, any web addresses or links contained in this book may have changed since publication and may no longer be valid. The views expressed in this work are solely those of the author and do not necessarily reflect the views of the publisher, and the publisher hereby disclaims any responsibility for them.

Any people depicted in stock imagery provided by Thinkstock are models, and such images are being used for illustrative purposes only. Certain stock imagery © Thinkstock.

ISBN: 978-1-4917-1235-1 (sc)
ISBN: 978-1-4917-1236-8 (hc)
ISBN: 978-1-4917-1237-5 (e)

Library of Congress Control Number: 2013919684

Printed in the United States of America.

iUniverse rev. date: 11/11/2013

Illustrations by Jo Spargo—Graphic Design and Illustration

Contents

Dedication vii
Acknowledgements xiii
Introduction xv

Chapter 1.   Bizarre Beginnings 1
Chapter 2.   First Impressions 9
Chapter 3.   The P.T.S. 16
Chapter 4.   Caring for the Kids 31
Chapter 5.   The Hospital Dance 40
Chapter 6.   On Violence 49
Chapter 7.   The Cinema 57
Chapter 8.   More Training 60
Chapter 9.   Living In 64
Chapter 10. The Chain Gang 83
Chapter 11. The Fire Brigade 92
Chapter 12. The Female Side of the Hospital 102
Chapter 13. Eurhythmics 108
Chapter 14. The Bath House 114
Chapter 15. Grace 118
Chapter 16. Sick Bay 120
Chapter 17. Sports Day 130
Chapter 18. The Refractory 136
Chapter 19. The Funeral 142
Chapter 20. Night Duty 149
Chapter 21. The Finals 167

Postscript 175
Appendix 1 181
Appendix 2 185

Dedication

My sincere and grateful thanks to Carol my wife, my encouragement and my editor; my supportive children Joanne the illustrator, Shelley the motivator and Gemma the carer; and to all those unsung hero's who worked and still work in mental health at the grass roots level. Thank you for your care, compassion, humour and for working in a service when no one else cared very much.

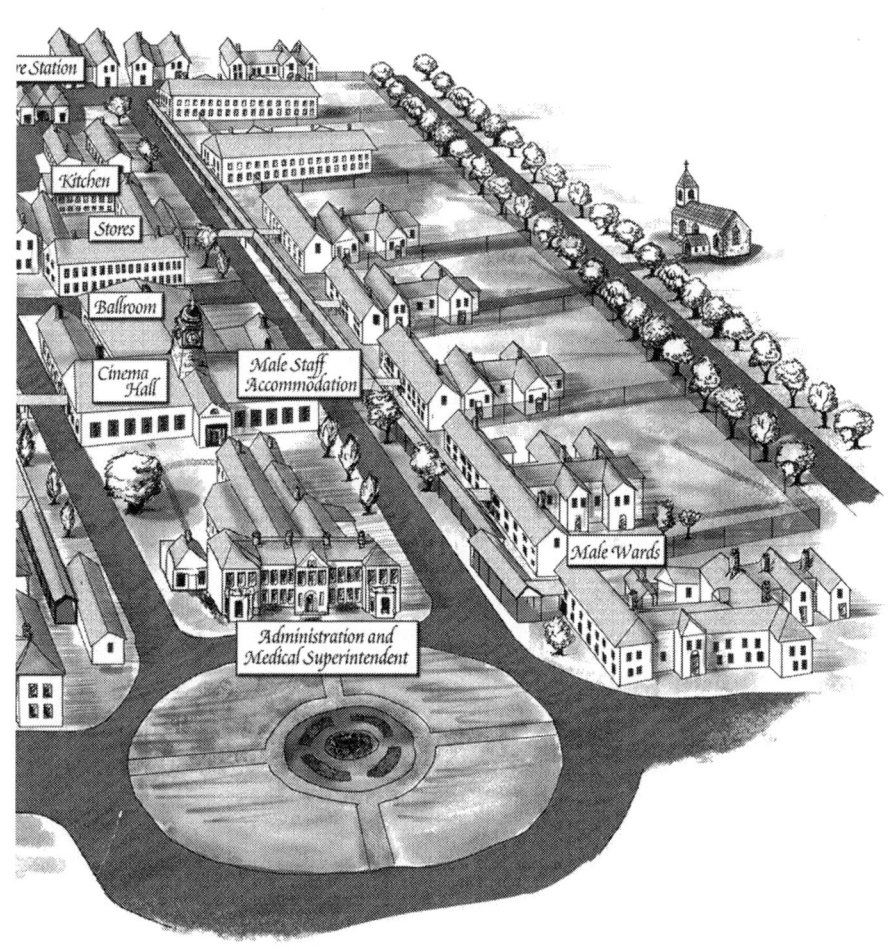

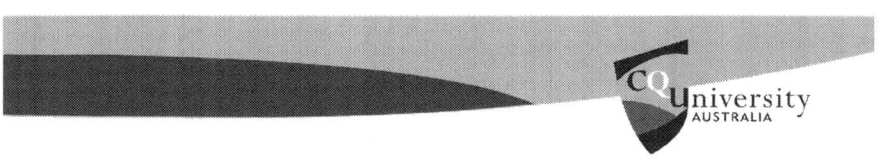

It give me great pleasure to write this foreword for a manuscript that I thoroughly enjoyed reading.

Gordon Kerkham begins *"Random Reflections of a Looney Bin"* by saying if we don't like the expression Looney Bin he doesn't give a flying fart. Well . . . I don't much like the expression but that is because the provision of contemporary mental health care has moved on from "lunatic asylum" days. The wave we ride these days is a Recovery Based model but having said that, years ago staff knew no better treatment methods and were trying to do the best they could under very difficult circumstances. Hindsight is a wonderful lens and I often ponder what future communities will say about care provided these days. Really, *Random Reflections of a Looney Bin* concentrates on the eccentricities of staff. The patients all appear very normal by comparison.

What this well written account of life at "Halley" gives us in the 21st century is a clear reminder of how institutionalisation affected not only the patients but also those who were there to provide care. Gordon's training days were a series of rights of passage, of unwritten rules and of a mental health nursing culture that did not base its approach, as it does today on evidence based practice, but largely one of survival.

Shocking at times because of its raw honesty, but written in an endearingly humorous and engaging manner, *Random Reflections of a Looney Bin*, is quite simply a bloody good read.

Dr. Lorna Moxham RN MHN PhD MED BhSc. FACMHN
Head of School of Nursing and Health Studies
Faculty of Arts Humanities and Education
Central Queensland University.

Acknowledgements

I would like to play tribute to the skills and patience of my Editor and wife Carol for the hours of pouring over drafts and correcting my outrageous spelling which spell check seems to miss. A great debt of thanks is owed to Joanne Spargo, of Graphic Design and Illustration for her fabulous art work. It is great to meet an illustrator who is always willing to change her work to meet the memories of the writer. Of course it helps if the author is her father. Thank you to my other daughters who always seem to have the knack to of being there to encourage "dad." Thank you Lorna Moxham for the forward and the shared memories of the good old days.

To my friends for their kind and supportive comments, encouragement and advice I say thank you most sincerely.

A special thank you needs to be said to all those whacky, wild, caring, dedicated and selfless individuals whom I have had the honour to work with over the years. I think we did the best with what we had.

Finally I must acknowledge the publishing team at iUniverse for their support, guidance and encouragement which helped enable me to turn my reflections into a readable book.

Gordon Kerkham, Author

Introduction

If you don't like the expression "Looney Bin" well tough 'cos I don't give a flying fart. That's what they were, that's what they are. You can dress them up with any name that you want but they will remain dumping grounds for all that we don't want to see or acknowledge in our world. This book is a true myth, that is, the reflections represent mostly the truth with some of the folklore and myth which accumulate through time. They are what I remember of my early training and work in a large institution for people with mental illness and /or intellectual disabilities.

I have had the opportunity to visit and work in many similar institutions to Halley in many parts of the world. As I talk to the staff, look at the building, and examine the attitudes. I have come to realise that institutions are the same the world over. It doesn't matter if it is for people with intellectual disabilities, the mentally ill or a twenty first century nursing home for the elderly. There are similarities in all of them.

So, if you know of, or work in an institution, be it for the aged, handicapped or psychiatric patients, and you think that you recognise some of the staff and situations, then you are probably right. It's your local institution on which these reflections are based.

It was in the early sixties that I went to work in my first institution. About the time of "Heartbeat" rock 'n' roll—Bill Halley, the Six Five Special and Bandbox. The point of this story is it happened and is still happening today in many parts of the civilised world.

In case the reader thinks that this tale cannot be true, that it didn't happen-and I must admit to thinking at times that my memory was playing tricks with me. I include an extract of the book of rules of Halley hospital as an appendix. But for now, join my world as I leave home and set out on this mind-bending journey.

Chapter 1

Bizarre Beginnings

Here I was, standing outside the front gate of Halley Hospital ready to start my career journey. I was tall for my seventeen years—but thin with it. With the exception of a passing interest in the school rugby team I had finished high school with little involvement in sport except as an interested spectator. Concentrated exposure to the lack of Manchester sunlight, my pale complexion and emaciated looks, led to my trendy lean and hungry looks while less than flattering friends called it death warmed up. Not that I was thin but it had even been suggested that if I stood sideways and put out my tongue I would look like a zip. I put these jibes aside because I was doing what none of my friends were. I had left home, left the security of the city, and come away on my own, to work. My father's words of advice, as he pushed a packet of 3 "Durex" contraceptives into the top pocket of my jacket as I left to catch the early bus, were still ringing in my ears.

"*You're old enough to know what those are for. Now don't bring any trouble home with you, it will only upset your mother.*"

The post war labour government's attempts to produce technologists had pushed me through an education system designed to turn out draftsmen, metal workers, scientists and electricians. The result of Government prompting brought out the anarchist in me and completely alienated me from all things commercial and industrial. Even at that early age I had learned not to trust politicians too much.

I developed, with prompting from a mother who seemed to have enough love to spare for the whole district, a naive urge to help people.

Having seen the life story of Helen Keller in the movie "*The Miracle Worker.*" I found myself a cause. The mentally handicapped, and with the full confidence of youth decided to be a "*miracle worker*" myself. Had I known my job description was to be titled "Male Nurse," and nursing in those male chauvinist pig dominated days being equated with all things feminine, I don't think I'd have started in the job.

My teenage image of nurses was purely sexual. To my mind, *"nurses are females with black stockings, aprons, frilly caps and perfume that makes the hair stand up on the back of my neck. They are the stuff of fantasies, wet dreams and the occasional smile from the top deck of a passing bus."* Ergo! nursing is certainly not the job for me.

Through a friend of the family I was supplied with information about a hospital serving the Manchester area and wrote away for application forms. It took what seemed an age for the recruiting package to arrive, but when it did it met all my expectations. There in the brown manila envelope was an idiot—proof application form and a beautifully illustrated brochure about Halley Hospital.

"The hospital is situated in the heart of the middle valley, two and a half miles from the picturesque village of Halley."

The words jumped out of the pages as I read about this wonderful employment opportunity.

There followed a series of photographs from the most advantageous angles, illustrating; the ballroom, with sprung maple floors; the badminton court; the dining rooms; the social club; staff bedrooms; the country walks; angling facilities on the stretch of river which ran through the hospital grounds; local bus services; theatre's in nearby towns and the tennis courts.

In addition the brochure waxed eloquently about the superb training facilities for staff; the free uniform and pension scheme. It sold me. Come hell or high water, this was where I was going to work.

Tucked away in an obscure corner of the brochure was the mere detail that two thousand five hundred patients were also involved with the Halley Hospital.

My first encounter with the hospital came on the day I arrived to start work. I had been interviewed several weeks earlier by the Chief Male Nurse but was in such a state of nervous excitement nothing had registered. Now, here I was standing outside the gates, suitcase in hand and set to challenge the world.

The sign said *"All persons must report to the gate-house."*

It was the sort of gate-house common on ministry of defense properties. Painted green with a long window looking out onto the drive it only needed a soldier in uniform. The window opened like a

British Rail ticket office window with a counter on the inside. Even the thin layer of grime and dust which always seemed to attached itself to the railway office windows was evident and I had to wipe myself a little peep hole to peer through.

Inside I saw a big cheerful fire in the grate. A dingy cream board full of hooks and numbers graced the far wall. From some of the hooks large bunches of keys rested. One or two of the key rings had what looked like police whistles attached. In an armchair in front of the fire was a man, toasting his boots and giving a good impression of being completely exhausted after a hard day's toil at the coal face. He was Bert Willis: The Guardian of the Gate.

Bert was dressed in his daily work clothes. White collarless shirt, navy trousers with World War One braces handed down by his father, and heavy black boots. A clean collar complete with studs and a tie was secreted in the drawer under the window. It was there for visiting days and the day the Board of Management was due to meet.

My rather tentative knocking did nothing for the inert figure sprawled in the armchair and it took a good few minutes of clattering the glass with a coin before I caught his attention and he opened the window

"Yes?" it was both a question and a statement. He thrust his face through the window—all boozy red and stubbled chin. Bert didn't like being disturbed out of what he considered office hours. His function was to issue keys to staff as they came on duty before 7.00 am and receive keys as they went off duty at 8.00 pm. Resident staff were taking a *"diabolical liberty"* if they came in or out of the hospital outside these times. I soon learned that, although it was against the rules, it was easier to keep your keys on your person as you went in and out during the evening than risk the wrath of Bert.

As this was my first confrontation with him I was a little taken aback at his abrupt manner. I felt myself colour-up and quickly handed him my letter of appointment.

Letters of appointment meant very little to Bert. If you were not in the daily appointment book it was hard to get in. I was logged in the book but I still had to suffer Bert's power ritual. He read and re-read my letter and then proceeded to ask me a barrage of questions.

"Where yer from?"

"What school'd ye go to?"

"Did ye father ever work ere?"

The questions came fast and furious and I found myself answering as though he was the headmaster of my old high school, adding a "Sir," at regular intervals as a mark of respect.

Eventually, having obtained my life history as far back as my great grandmother, assured himself I was not going to blow up the Medical Superintendents office, and phoned up the "Chief's" office to make sure they were expecting me, my letter was returned and I was allowed to enter the grounds.

I'd broken my ties with home and friends to become a ward orderly/student nurse and it was too late to back out now. I had been told I was lucky to be appointed, as the minimum age for nursing was 18 years and so for the first year they'd found a special classification for me. Apparently I was the youngest person the institution had employed and I suspect that I would have been turned away if it had not been for the political clout of my family friend.

The administration buildings was at the end of a mile long, tree-lined drive. Despite the crispness of this autumn morning I was perspiring by the time I arrived at the chief male nurses office. The thick, noise deadening carpet of autumn leaves on the path made it a silent journey where every nut falling from a tree heralded an out of control inmate about to leap out and get me. Even with my heavy suitcase to contend with I was almost running by the time I reached the sanctuary of the administration building.

The chief male nurse who had interviewed me several weeks earlier was away sick, his deputy was on leave and the senior assistant chief male nurse was in charge.

"Leave thy case 'ere lad." He indicated with a nod of his head towards the far corner of his office. "Routine first, then we'll find you a room." The man raised his portly figure from behind his desk and started putting on a peaked uniform hat as he spoke.

"Medical first."

Although he was a big, heavy looking, man he moved fast and he passed me and was out of the office door heading towards an open sided covered walkway. I had to put on a spurt to catch him up. The staff medical was carried out on a ward, which doubled as the infirmary for all the male residents in the institution. It was to this location that I was being led. On the way to our destination I learned that my guide's name was Alf Stone and that all the male wards were off this long corridor.

Any hopes I had of instant patient contact, so I could start my miracle working, were dashed when he informed me I wouldn't be allowed to work on the wards proper until I reached the age of eighteen. My duties up to that time would be to work as a general help in the chiefs' office. Our one sided conversation was brought to an abrupt end as Alf halted in front of green double doors.

"This is ward one," he said. "That's ward two," he indicated a second identical set of doors.

How will I ever remember, I thought with a sinking feeling in the pit of my stomach. There were no nameplates, no signs, in fact, nothing in the external appearance of the wards to denote any difference one from another.

Taking an enormous bunch of keys on a long key chain from out of his pocket, Alf selected one and unlocked the ward door. He didn't seem to feel the need to explain why all the doors were locked. Once through the door Alf closed and locked it behind us.

We were in a long corridor, bare of any furniture and made distinctive only by its lack of windows and highly polished wooden floor. The illumination for the corridor came from lights shining from behind the frosted glass panels in another set of double doors at the end of the passage. I could detect movement behind the glass but couldn't make out any shape or form. There was a plain wooden door in the middle side of the corridor to our right and it was to this that Alf steered me. Everything was silent and seemed to inhibit conversation so I stood quietly while my guide selected yet another key from his chain, opened up and led me through.

It was a conventional examination room with couch, scales, x-ray reading viewer and a series of trays containing the usual paraphernalia for examining the human body. Just like the doctor's surgery back home.

"Strip down to your underpants and hop on the couch, I'll tell 'em that your here." Alf turned and left the room and I heard him unlocking the double doors at the end of the corridor.

There was a slight burst of noise and then all fell silent again. I stripped and sat on the edge of the couch. I was glad mum had bought me those new underpants and I'd put them on that morning. I sat for an age in that oppressive silence until I heard the unlocking of the door again. Alf's head appeared round it giving me a start.

"The doctor will be along soon. Come back to the office afterwards. Oh! And do him a specimen of wee in that jar if you can." He indicated a glass jar at the sink.

Just as quickly he was gone and I heard him unlocking and locking the outer door. I had no trouble providing the specimen, nervous anticipation saw to that. I sat back on the examination couch. Silence and then more silence. Ideas began to force their way into my mind. *I was locked on a ward in a mental hospital with no clothes on. What if they thought I was an inmate?*

I was relieved of my depressing thoughts as I heard footsteps padding down the corridor. Strange, I hadn't heard it unlock this time. The footsteps came nearer and then passed the door and receded. No, they were coming back. The pad padding halted outside the door and slowly it opened. A cold clammy fear clutched at me—it was hard to breath, I could feel my pulse racing and I am sure my heart was trying to leap out of my chest. I could have filled that urine flask all over again.

There, framed in the doorway stood a bizarre-looking man. He had, a domed balding head and staring eyes which were too big for their sockets. A fine stubble of two or three days without shaving was on his chin and little tufts of hair sprouted unevenly where the razor had repeatedly missed. His jacket was crumpled and his shirt collar was open half inside and half outside his coat. His baggy un-pressed trousers finished just above his ankles and odd socks terminated in well-worn carpet slippers. My young head was still filled with the popular images of the mentally ill, Quasimodo, Frankenstein and wild eyed Hitchcock's Psycho's with the strength of ten men. I steeled myself expecting his sudden pounce, screwed up my eyes and offered up prayers to an unseen God.

"You're the person for the medical? I'm Dr.Davids. Have you managed a specimen?"

I gasped with relief and clutched at the side of the examination couch surreptitiously wiping my sweaty palms on the sheet beneath me and nodding assent to the doctor. The door opened again and Dr. Davids was joined by a tall, distinguished looking man wearing a white coat. It was full length and cut in the style used by dentists giving him a very professional appearance. He was clean-shaven, well groomed with hair neatly styled and smelled of Old Spice, after shave. Under his arm he carried a clip-board, report and charts.

The man promptly busied himself setting up weighing machines and a device for measuring height. I had, like most boys of my age, talked about poofs, but I'd never met one. With no frame of reference to guide me, I just put his clipped mincing gait down to his professional manner. *'In the early '60's the word gay just meant happy and camp was what one did in the woods.'*

"Hop on the scales—love." He smiled, displaying a small fortune in gold fillings. As he set about the task of efficiently measuring and recording my height and weight.

"Ever been sick love?"

"No." I coughed nervously as I noticed Dr. David standing in the corner of the room watching me with his head cocked to one side. The male nurse made some more notes on his chart. Then, turning to look at the doctor asked softly with a slight lisp.

"Any questions?"

I didn't discern any movement from the doctor he just stood looking at me as the male nurse said:

"Well, that's it, get dressed and I'll let you out."

I'd always been a quick dresser. You learn to be when you experience a cold northern winter with ice on the inside of the bedroom windows and no central heating. But on this occasion I broke all records.

The male nurse, metal heels clip clopping on the wooden floors led the way to the door where I'd entered the ward. Opening it with a key attached to a long chain which disappeared somewhere in the folds of his gown. He stood back to let me pass. Without warning he flashed his expensive smile at me again and nodded towards the walls of the corridor. For the first time I noticed they were painted a sickly yellow.

"Like the colour scheme?" he pouted, "I chose it myself."

Before I could reply. He winked, propelled me on to the corridor and closed the ward door behind me. Assuming the medical to be over I hurried along the corridor desperately seeking the comparative safety of Alf in the office.

The next few hours were a kaleidoscope of impressions. I received my uniform from the stores; I was shown the dining room; received a bunch of keys of my own (which I had to sign for in a large book and was admonished to remember the number embossed thereon for the gate) and finally was taken to a room on the first floor of the resident male staff quarter called the staff block.

My door key opened my room and only my room, yet it would also open all male ward doors in the hospital. Alf deposited me at the door.

"Number 56, same as your key number."

He smiled,

"Well lad, spend the rest of the day unpacking and looking round. Time enough to start work in the morning. Report to the office at nine o clock first day."

He moved off towards the stairs that led back to his office. I closed the door behind me and surveyed my room. Bed, wardrobe, dressing table, writing desk, armchair, linen on the bed waiting to be made up, towels behind the door. It was like a hotel room in movies I'd seen. I crossed and looked outside the window. The view overlooked the open sided corridor and the place was beginning to come alive with staff purposefully moving about their duties.

I could feel excitement welling up inside me. *I'd started work, I'd done it, I'd bloody done it—I was going to be a miracle worker.*

Chapter 2

First Impressions

So began my working life at the Halley hospital. As I said earlier they'd never employed one so young before and the nursing officers were at a loss what to do with me. I was legally too young to work on the wards and in the end the chief male nurse decided to keep me in the office as a messenger for himself and the senior nursing officers. My duties entailed getting into the office in the morning before the chiefs started, usually before seven-o-clock, lighting the fire, tidying their desks and then polishing the floor.

The hospital didn't possess a polishing machine and all the floors were kept in gleaming condition by means of a device called a "bumper." It was a brick of 28 lb. of lead set in a wooden block. It had a bristle base and pivoted on a long wooden staff. On the wards the 'bumper' also served as an excellent means of control for potentially aggressive and antisocial or hyper-active patients. The easy fix of mind bending drugs was not an option for these institutions. The aggression and energy required to swing a 28 lb. lead floor polisher left one glassy eyed and exhausted. In the days before sedation it must have inhibited countless acts of violence.

I found all this cleaning a bit hard to take. I'd come into the health service with youthful dreams of curing the afflicted not to clean an office. I would console myself, by remembering it was only for a year and then I would be on the wards caring for real people. Later on I was to find that many of the ward duties were this same task of cleaning only it was disguised by being called nursing.

Working in the office not only stood me in good stead in later years, but it gave me a special relationship with most of the senior nursing staff. To them I was known as 'Gordon lad' and during the year each

Sub (short for sub officer) used some of the time to pass on the benefit of his wisdom.

"Gordon lad, always carry a duster in your back pocket and when you see someone important, or looking important, polish the nearest thing to you. You'll soon earn the reputation of being a good worker.— By the way—sub officers are important."

"You're the most junior person in the place so if you can't remember someone's name just call them Sir and you'll be right. You could probably get away with calling the female matron Sir as well."

"Ah! Lad, this is the numbers board. We record all the patients on it."

Males	1250 Residents	Status	Total
License	28	Voluntary	500
Leave	12	Compulsory	700
Farm	10	Epileptics	500

I had wondered what this list of figures was for standing pride of place in the office.

"It looks good but it's not accurate. Numbers are always changing and by the time we put one on the board it's changed again. So! Gordon lad. Whenever you're out with a group and a senior officer asks, *"How many patients are with you?"* Give him a number. It doesn't matter if it's the right one, an approximate one will do. That way you'll always appear on top of the job."

I came to realise that to many of the senior staff the patients in bulk were merely numbers. The only ones who had names were those who performed some task. They served tea, ran away, were aggressive, cleaned shoes, or undertook some other task of service like digging their gardens'.

There were times when I think I had an inhibiting effect on the natural dialogue of the office. On many occasions one of the subs would start to swear and break off in mid sentence when they realised 'the lad' was present. It was not that I had a particularly sheltered upbringing and swearing was not unknown to me. But, like so many of the "Heartbeat-Buddy Holly" generation I didn't hear adults swear very often and never on films and television. Even when an adult did swear it was usually a mild expletive. Only once did I hear one of the subs in full cry.

I was quietly checking the night time clock in the office and he must have forgotten I was there when he received a directive from the medical administration that he patently disagreed with. It was like a low rumble at first slowly rising to a crescendo.

"Never have so fucking many.
Been fucked about
by so fucking few.
For so fucking long
for so fucking little"

I cowered in the corner as he stormed out of the room waving the offending memo in his hand. I was hoping and praying he hadn't seen me and quietly stored his Churchillian outburst away in my golden treasury of swearing for all occasions.

Although there were six sub officers the male nursing administration was really influenced by two people, Bill and Alf. The chief male nurse went off on long term sick leave shortly before I started work. This left the whole of the male side of the institution to the tender mercies of his deputy who was promoted to act as chief during his absence.

'Bill the bastard', as he was not so affectionately known was qualified mainly by virtue of experience. A series of grandfather clauses in industrial awards had given him an impressive series of letters after his name that would take the modern students many years of study and hard work to obtain.

Deputy Bill was a small man standing just five feet tall and of slight build. It was surprising he'd ever managed to find a place in the mental health service because, when he started work at Halley in the 1930's there was wholesale unemployment in the north and only the fittest and tallest men got through the gates. However, there he was, and there to stay.

He suffered from small man syndrome and had chip on his shoulder, which was only just outshone by the two silver pips on each epaulette of his uniform jacket. Bill would strut, rather than walk, up and down the hospital corridors dressed in immaculate uniform of, highly polished shoes, whiter than white shirt, blacker than black tie and socks. The creases in his uniform trousers would have sliced through his limbs if he'd worn them inside out. The shine on his boots was only fractionally outdone by the mirror patent leather of his peaked cap. He even went so far as to remove his cap by the crown rather than risk getting fingerprints on the brim. Bill seemed in love with the service side of mental health and wearing his uniform as a shield he judged others by their 'turn-out' rather than their deeds.

Along with many of his contemporaries, Bill joined the service when custodial care was the order of the day and he hadn't been able to adjust to the challenge of the sixties. About half the patients in the hospital were detained through an order of the courts and needed to be accounted for in his mysterious book of numbers. Like the numbers board in the office, the individual had no name but was an object to be accounted for like the ward inventory of equipment.

From not having to know patient's names, Bill even managed to get by without learning those of his staff. Everyone who was subordinate he called "Mister" and all superiors were called "Sir." This caused him occasional embarrassment when he was confronted with a stranger who may be a new member of the nursing staff and could be comfortably called mister or may be a new doctor in which case a Sir was called for. He would studiously avoid the others gaze and wait for them to speak first hoping that they would give him a clue as to how to address them. I only once saw him caught out. He *"Sir'd"* a well dressed but mute mentally handicapped patient all the way down to one of the wards only to find out the guy was being informally admitted. Wow! He was so new, he didn't even deserve a place in the numbers book.

Following all the 'right and proper' rules of his conduct Bill would never give a member of staff a 'choking-off' in front of the patients, or even another member of staff. Often the first you knew of his proximity was a light tap on the shoulder.

"A word in your ear mister." He'd say and walk away. Your role was to follow him a dutiful distance behind like a servile eastern woman following her husband. When Bill judged you were out of earshot of anyone who might listen. He'd stop and turn round for you to catch up.

His pet hate was staff wearing non-regulation ties closely followed by the unforgivable sin of not having your keys on the key chain. The rules held that the key chain had to be visible below the bottom of the jacket to prove it was being worn. Attached to the chain should be your ward key and whistle for emergency use. The problem with heavy keys in trousers pockets is they wear holes and cause friction against the thigh when walking. Most of the staff took the keys off the chain and carried them in their jacket pocket.

Bill would demand to see the keys. A first offense of 'no keys on a chain' was a telling off. The threat the second time was "*down the road.*" The euphemism for the sack. You didn't get caught a third time.

Bill had the reputation of being entirely humourless—I once saw him smile although I admit it was a rare sight.

Several of the fifty or so resident male staff, mostly student nurses, owned motorbikes and were in the habit of going out for a drink in the evenings to the village pub. We'd set off after work at about eight thirty, in convoy. I didn't own a bike, but was a regular pillion passenger on my neighbour Franks' bike. The most direct route took us out of the back gate, avoiding Bert and his keys, then past one of the rows of houses on the hospital staff housing estate; houses which were built around the perimeter of the grounds for married staff.

During the evening down the pub the group would split up. Some would go pulling birds, some to play cards, dominoes or darts and others to concentrate on serious drinking. Occasionally we would meet up again at the local fish and chip shop, when the pub closed, to compare notes before returning to the hospital.

The morning after one of the more noisy exits from the hospital, when we students had all managed to set off together, fourteen were summonsed to Bill's office. We assembled outside his door in single file so not to crowd the corridor, and waited his pleasure. It was a bit like being in school again and being sent to stand outside the headmaster's office. When at last Bill decided to see 'the offenders', the anticipation had created the desired sense of awe/fear. Remaining in Indian-file we trooped into the office. Bill calmly but emphatically explained the noise of the motorbikes passing his house in the evening displeased him. The group was threatened with "severe consequences" if such a thing were to happen again.

Once our group got over its shock we became indignant and angry. That night saw seven motorbikes complete with seven pillion passengers set off on their village bound journey from the resident staff quarters. As the bikes approached number 5 the Avenue, where Bill lived, the throaty roar of the engines suddenly ceased and rolled to a halt. One by one, fourteen motorcyclists dismounted and pushing our machines tiptoed past the gate. At number 6 we remounted, revved our engines and thundered off into the night.

The next morning saw our group called to the office again and this time feeling very apprehensive as the courage from the night before deserted us. We were going to get it for sure. Bill stood up as we entered and we must have visibly cowered. He smiled.

"Point taken gentlemen. You may go back on duty."

We walked from his office in a state of shock. Not only were we gentlemen—he had smiled. Really smiled. The old bastard was human after all. Still, none of us students was game to try that stunt again and the revelers risked the wrath of Bert at the front gate after that.

In stark contrast with Bill was Alf. As the senior chief nursing officer he became acting deputy during the tenure of Bill at the top. A frustrated railway engineer he'd been driven to join the institution for employment during the industrial depression and risen to his present position through some thirty years of persistent plodding. His heart however, remained with his railways and when he thought no one was looking would gaze for hours at the cut-away drawings of locomotives which were the popular centerfold of the boys 'Eagle' comic. He'd buy the comic each week on his way to work—ostensibly for the resident who cleaned his shoes. The resident always got the comic, but without the center page. Great was Alf's disappointment the week they featured an aeroplane instead of one of his beloved trains.

Alf was as large as Bill was short. Portly, beer potted, unhurried and apparently unconcerned. Alf brought an air of sanity into the hospital environment.

When a patient absconded most people panicked. Staff were sent running in all directions to search for the offender. Search parties were organised and people would hare off all over the place. Not when Alf was on duty. He would leisurely reach over, pick up the phone and give a complete description of the runaway to the local police—often from memory.

"Hello Charlie, We've one away. Aye it's Titch Hanson. You'll find him waiting at the X23 bus stop. You can't miss him he'll still be wearing his white jacket. He works in the kitchen and the silly bugger won't have the sense to take it off. He'll be trying to go home to his mum. Pick him up and bring him back will you before my colleagues all have seizures."

Invariably he would be right. Being a creature of habit he had an empathy with those people who habitually ran away.

Alf's favorite expression was "Ah! Th'eel be Reet." Obliging in the extreme it soon became obvious when Alf was on duty and Bill was off. A long queue of nursing staff would quickly form outside the office patiently waiting to have their off duty roster changed. Most people asked for the weekend off and were met with Alf's affable "Thee'l be Reet."

As a consequence the hospital was staffed for the weekend on a frantic Friday with overtime for anyone who would work. This usually fell to the student nurses and assistants as trained staff found it uneconomical to work a flat rate overtime.

During my time as the office boy Alf offered me much sound advice but none better than that which he gave on the first day I was allowed to work on a ward following the PTS training. I'd reported on duty, on the children's ward, which was not unknown to me. I was feeling very proud now I was a first year student nurse.

My ego was quickly dented when the charge nurse gave me some routine cleaning tasks far removed from the children. The jobs were so trivial they only took me an hour to complete. I was in the act of reporting back to the charge for something else to do, secretly hoping he would let me go and do something with the patients.

When Alf walked into the ward the charge nurse was giving forth in amazement that I'd completed my appointed tasks so quickly. I gathered that the charge had been hoping that I'd at least be out of his hair until the end of the morning. New staff always cluttered up the place and spoiled the harmony of inactivity by asking questions. Grasping the situation instantly Alf took me to one side. "What time do you come on duty son?"

"Seven o clock sir."

"And what time do you go off tonight?"

"Eight o clock, sir."

"Ah! Well, Gordon lad, always remember tha's got 'till eight oclock. Pace tha' self."

He plodded off down the corridor and with a rattle of keys left the ward. All his life Alf paced himself. The great unflappable he eventually received an M.B.E. for his services to the mentally handicapped. He deserved it if only for spending forty years in the same hospital. Forty years of persistent plodding.

Chapter 3

The P.T.S.

My eighteenth birthday approached, towards the end of my first year in the hospital. I was sent by the Subs to the nurse training school for an interview with the principal tutor. The common practice in most institutions was that all students attended a preliminary training school, called P.T.S. before being let loose on the wards. I was, subject to my interview, to be part of the school's next intake.

I must admit I was quite excited at the prospect of getting into some training. I was still determined to be a *"miracle worker"* although I was gradually beginning to settle for just getting through the day. For the last few months the chiefs had released me from office duties during the afternoons and allowed me to work on the children's ward. Of course, I wasn't allowed officially to work with the patients, only cleaning duties but the *"Nelsons eye"* of the charge allowed me to assist with the severely physically and intellectually disabled children in the dormitory from time to time. I was encouraged with the thought that in six weeks time I would be able to get involved officially.

The training school was situated in a converted ward above the female infirmary. When students were in the school was the only time that male staff could be seen in evidence on the female side of the hospital. It wasn't permissible to cut through the corridors of the administration building in order to attend the school. Students had to walk the long way round outside the buildings. It was most enjoyable on a warm autumn morning but was to become a considerable trudge on the cold, wet winter days which were to follow. I'd only visited the female side of the hospital once before. Taking a message to Matron from the chief male nurse. I couldn't wait to get back from that petticoat dominated world to the security of the all-male environment I worked in. Such was the effect of enforced segregation of patients that it spun off into the staff lives as well. At least during on duty hours. This enforced apartheid made it very difficult for male staff to relate to their female counterparts on a professional basis. After duty hours in the staff social club was another matter.

The first thing that struck me about the school was the smell. It looked like a ward on the outside but there was none of the mixture of odours, which made up a ward. There was no smell of too many bodies compressed into too little space, no smell of stale urine, no hint of faeces, nor the occasional paraldehyde, no excessive use of Dettol and floor polish. Instead the school was clean and fresh with a gentle hint of spring flowers.

The corridor still had the appearance of a ward only without the trappings of habitation. The outside door wasn't locked. Although this was only because the male tutor wasn't allowed a key which would also open female wards. The building was secured at night by one of the Assistant matrons on her rounds. The whole place had a functional atmosphere. What would have been dormitories were classrooms, side rooms were study cubicles or offices, the day room was a practical area with beds and a long table covered with surgical instruments. Stainless steel trolleys were in evidence. All set up to perform hypothetical procedures on hypothetical people. The charge nurses' office bore the legend "Principal Tutor." I knocked.

"Come in." The voice was clear and young sounding

I entered cautiously. I knew Mr. Thomas by reputation from my conversations with resident students. None of them had ever referred to Mr. Thomas by his Christian name. In fact none of them seemed to know it. There was a sort of cautious note to voices when they mentioned his name aloud. The figure sitting behind the desk lived up to all my expectations. He was a man in his mid thirties with fair, neatly groomed wavy hair, bright blue eyes, clean-shaven with a fresh country boy complexion. He sat with a very upright bearing, hands with clean manicured fingernails were clasped in front of him. He was wearing the same uniform as the Sub Officers—with one pip—and it looked far more dashing on his youthful figure. I'd taken considerable care with my own appearance for this first interview having been warned about Mr. Thomas's pre-occupation with uniforms.

The Chief's gave me very little information about the training school. It was, after all, situated on the female side of the hospital and a place of learning. It intruded into the rostering system of staff because students needed time off to attend lectures but other than that it was another world.

I stood just inside the doorway while his blue eyes ran me up and down. There was no trace of an expression on his face, but my carefully pressed trousers, clean shirt, highly polished shoes and the fact I was wearing my peaked uniform cap must have passed muster.

"Sit down nurse"

It was the first time I'd been called nurse since I'd arrived at the hospital and it took me aback. I was so used to the "*Mister*" of the wards or the "Gordon Lad" of the office that the expression needed some time to register. Mr. Thomas called everyone nurse. It was his first step in your training. There were no personalities, no gender just professional nurses.

The interview was conducted very formally. I was asked about educational attainments, interests hobbies and girl friends. I answered the questions as well as I could but couldn't help thinking most of it was a waste of time. For, lying on the desk in front of Mr. Thomas was my staff file, with all the relevant information contained within its buff coloured covers. I knew that the interview was concluded when he closed the file in front of him with a snap.

"Very good. You can start in the P.T.S. Which begins a week on Monday. Lectures start at eight thirty sharp. You will need pens, ruler, pencils, three exercise books hard backed and the first five text books from this reading list."

Mr. Thomas, still unsmiling, handed me a typewritten foolscap sheet listing the schools reading requirements and with a nod of his head, dismissed me.

I left the office and gently closed the door behind me. I'd mixed feelings, elated at the start of my career training, but deflated at the treatment I'd just received from the principal tutor. He was far more formidable than any of the teachers I remembered from my secondary school days. Still, I was going to start training.

The first day of the P.T.S. arrived and I reported to the school with my brand new text books and writing materials all assembled in a shiny plastic briefcase bought especially for the occasion. There were twenty students in the group and we were evenly divided—ten of each sex—an administrative nicety.

It was a strange feeling, like the first day in a new school. New pads, new pens, new faces. None of the faces were familiar to me although one or two of the males gave me a nod as I entered. It occurred to me that I'd a slight advantage over my new colleagues because most of them were starting work that day whereas I'd already been at the hospital for a whole year. The one or two men who'd nodded probably recognised my face from when they had attended their interviews at the Chief Male Nurse's office. The girls too were going through the same processes but none of them would have been near my working world.

It was like the first day in any new group situation. We stood in a compact mass recognizing that we were all in this together but all avoiding speaking or making eye contact with one another. Occasionally one of us would break the silence by asking a general question of anyone game enough to pick it up, for the most part though we retained a guarded silence with our secret thoughts. I had met a few female nurses in the pub and staff club during the evenings but at those times they were out of uniform and just like other girls. These were different and looked almost antiseptic in their starched aprons and caps. Some with just a hint of make-up and heady perfume that asserted their femininity despite the uniform.

Mr. Thomas appeared at his office door at exactly half past eight and our mute group turned expectantly towards him. He had the inevitable brown manila folder tucked under his arm.

"Come this way nurses." He did not request, he commanded, although there was nothing aggressive about his manner. I detected a ripple of anticipation run through the group as we followed him into a lecture room.

Once we were seated in the room Mr. Thomas gave us his introductory lecture. It was more like a seaside landlady laying down the rules to her guests.

- We would stand up when a tutor of nursing or a visiting lecturer entered the room.
- We would stand and give our name when answering a question.
- We would never, when in uniform, fold our arms in front of us.

- Full uniform, including hats, would be worn at all times when in school.
- Male nurses would carry their hats when inside the building.
- Failure to comply with the uniform rule would mean being sent back to the residences to put on correct dress and thereby miss the lecture.
- Once a lecture had commenced no one would be allowed to enter. Students arriving late would have to sit outside and make up their notes in their own time.
- After P.T.S. was over and we had been allocated to wards offending students would be returned to that ward to work during that lecture period.
- Notes had to be taken at all lectures unless instructed otherwise.
- All notes had to be written up clearly in our exercise books and handed in each Friday evening for marking.

I sat open-mouthed not really believing what I was hearing. The expressions on the faces of my colleagues verified my feelings. Some of the group was obviously mature student entrants into training and yet here we were being treated like less than first year secondary school students. There was not even a second for us to discuss the introductory talk as Mr. Thomas led straight into his first lecture.

We were inundated with quantities of paper. Timetables, rules and collections of question some 300 to a set covering various aspects of nursing. Mr. Thomas had reduced nursing education to its lowest common denominator—questions and answers.

Our first subject was "Ventilation and the ward" during which the system was briefly explained to us. On the first sheet of paper we had a list of questions on the subject to which Mr. Thomas would dictate the answers. Each morning we would have a test where he would ask each student a random question from the previous days list. We had better get it right.

The rest of the session was spent frantically writing down answers to questions at dictation speed. Finally morning coffee break came to relieve the tension. Gone was the mute group of the early morning. Although the hallowed sanctum of the school tended to make people talk in whispers—they were angry indignant whispers.

"Who does he think he is?"

"We're not bloody kids."

"Jesus! it was never like this in high school."

There was a silence as the group looked to our obviously older colleagues for advice. Derek was the one who spoke.

"We used to have instructors like that in the army. You can't change them, they do it all by the book. So, if you want to qualify just do it his way. You can always forget it afterwards and its only three years."

"Yes." added Roy, the more taciturn of the two men, "don't let the bastard grind you down."

The bell calling us back into the classroom ended further discussion. It was only eleven-o clock on our first day in school and already we were getting disenchanted.

The next lecture was from the only other permanent tutor in the school. Mr. Sandy. He was several years junior to Mr. Thomas and seemed considerably constrained by the relationship that the principal tutor expected him to keep with the students. Their relationship was further strained because Mr. Sandy was one of that unfortunate group of individuals who just do not look right in a uniform. He appeared with one side of the collar of his jacket turned up, eight inches of shirt cuff protruding from below his sleeve and trousers which looked as though they had been slept in. A thin film of chalk dust seemed to settle on him wherever he went, just like iron filings are attracted to a magnet.

We dutifully stood up as he entered and he bid us sit down with a wave of his hand. Any hopes we had of a respite from Mr. Thomas teaching style were dashed when Mr. Sandy's method was revealed. His approach was to read his subject from a textbook at dictation speed and we were expected to take these pearls of wisdom down in our note books word for word.

The only breaks we got from the incessant writing was when one of the students halted his flow to question the spelling of a word. Mr. Sandy was to be our tutor for the rest of the day and subject after subject passed before us at dictation speed. By afternoon tea we were all looking forward to the final session. It was timetabled as practical and by this time anything would be better than that interminable writing.

Mr. Thomas returned to teach practical nursing and we all followed him into the practical room with some trepidation. The row of gleaming surgical instruments and stainless steel trolleys that I had seen on my first visit to the school were still there and looked more intimidating than ever. We were to find out later that very few of these instruments could be found on the wards and that practical nursing was therefore divided into two parts, procedures as taught and procedures as practiced.

"First things first," said Mr. Thomas. "Before you can carry out any task you must first learn how to handle the equipment. For the next few weeks there will be one practical session each day when you will learn the name of five new instruments. You will also learn the correct way to make a hospital bed. At the end of your preliminary training you will know the names of all the common instruments and be able to make a bed to my standard."

"Bloody 'ell," muttered Roy in a stage whisper," I might as well 'av stayed in the army."

During that first week we learned nothing about the mentally handicapped and disordered people we were going to be caring for on the wards but, we did learn a lot about instruments and beds. The instruments were taught the same way as all the other nursing subjects. Mr. Thomas showed us the instrument and repeated its name and function a few times and the next day we were tested at random to see if we could recall the name.

For the first couple of days this was relatively easy but, as time went on the number of possible answers increased and so did the odds of making an error.

The days started to fly by as we struggled with a kaleidoscope of new facts that were presented to us. Mr. Thomas's tests became a thing of dread as the number of new concepts grew and the list of possible test questions got longer. Most of the group adopted a strategy of taking an early evening tea, bashing the books for an hour, and then joining with the rest of the group for a drink in the staff club and a post-mortem on the day.

We were quickly becoming an identifiable set within the confines of the hospital. All, that is, with the exception of Roy. He seemed to be finding the studying more and more difficult as the days passed. Some of us tried to coach him but he was rapidly losing interest and it was becoming apparent that he would not pass the final P.T.S. examination at the end of our six weeks.

Mr. Thomas was a hard taskmaster and only wanted successful students. I couldn't make up my mind whether this was for the good of the profession, where he only wanted a high standard of graduate to guarantee a high standard of care for the patients, or whether it was because students who fail reflect on his abilities as a tutor and cast doubts on his methods. Sadly I concluded that the latter was his motive.

By the Wednesday of the second week he had already carpeted Roy in the office and berated him over his poor performance. By the Friday it was decided that Roy would return to the wards as an unqualified orderly and return to the school at a later day when he'd done some preparatory study. Most of us in the group knew his return was unlikely and that historically students whom this happened to never came back. They either left the hospital or became untrained nurse assistants.

Coupled with our reluctance and sadness at seeing Roy leave there was a slight tinge of envy. He would be getting to work with the patients before any of us and we'd still have the hurdle of the examinations before us.

In the end Roy accelerated the seal on his own fate. In one gallant gesture he terminated his tenure in school and struck a blow for freedom on behalf of his new found friends. It was question time on the Friday morning of the fourth week. Mr. Thomas was standing at the front of the class firing his questions at random. Nurses were bobbing up and down like yo-yos with their rote answers.

"What is milk nurse?"

Helen, a very attractive blonde nurse stood up. "A white nutritious liquid secreted by the mammary glands of some female animals. It is produced to feed their infants. Common examples are humans, cows, pigs and goats."

This stock answer pleased Mr. Thomas and he dismissed Helen to her seat with a smile and a wave of his hand.

"Where do we store milk nurse?" The pointing finger indicated Roy.

Slowly, with a malevolent glint in his eye Roy rose from his chair. "In bottles."

The frown, which fluttered across Mr. Thomas brow, showed that this was not the answer that he wanted.

"Come now nurse," he said in an imperious tone, "You know that the correct answer is in a fridge at a temperature of 40 degrees Fahrenheit."

"Well!" Said Roy, warming to his theme. "You'd look pretty bloody silly pouring your milk into a fridge instead of a bottle. But that's the trouble with this training school, it bears no relationship to reality. I'm off to the wards where I can do some real good."

All of the time that he was talking Roy was gathering up his books and making for the door. He paused in the doorway and with a last look at us, his colleagues of only four weeks, said smiling.

"I'll be back."

And then he was gone. Gone to work in the wards until some vague future fate would give him a more patient chance. Mr. Thomas stood open-mouthed staring at the empty doorway. His fair complexion was whiter than ever. He made a little start as if to go after Roy but then thought the better of it and turned back to face the expectant class.

"Open your anatomy books at the skeletal system and get on with some private study. There will be a test on it this afternoon."

He walked quickly from the room leaving us for the first time to our own devices.

Mr. Sandy took the lessons for the rest of that day.

After that the days in the training school seemed to accelerate. We continued to spend less time with Mr. Thomas and more with Mr. Sandy and his text book dictation. Other lectures were introduced. The finance department, engineers, fire and safety and lastly the doctors. The experiences raced by. We learned a new professional language, anatomy and physiology, sickness and health, the Mental Health Act., the nature of mental handicaps and lots of practical nursing skills. We learned to say long words like sphygmomanometer and practiced dropping them into conversations at any opportunity. Every subject was introduced at an elementary level as a preparation for a study of the subjects in depth over the three years, which was to follow. The aim of this initial study was to give us sufficient skill and knowledge for us to be of some use on the wards we would eventually be allocated to. At the time it seemed like an endless treadmill of lectures, books, the staff club and bed.

Just when it seemed to be going on forever the end of P.T.S. examinations were upon us.

We learned the examinations were to be held over three days. There would be four written papers: Anatomy and Physiology and a Nursing Paper set by the tutors, a paper on the mental health act set by the doctor, drugs by the pharmacist and then, horror of horrors—a practical examination by the Matron.

In my experience there is nothing more calculated to make strong men go weak at the knees than the confrontation of a nursing practical examination by Matron. Particularly when it is conducted by a figure as awesome and formidable as 'Hell fire Harriet' the matron of Halley Hospital. For the male nurses who knew we didn't have to work under her administration she presented an added threat.

It was well known on the hospital grapevine that she'd scant regard for the male side of the institution and only spoke to the senior male nursing staff when it was absolutely necessary. This just added to our worries and became a frequent subject for discussion in the male staff common room in the days leading up to the examinations.

The written papers were taken on the Wednesday and Thursday of the final week of block and the practicals were scheduled for the Friday morning. Friday afternoon we would be given our results and ward allocations.

We had arranged a party in the staff club afterwards to drown sorrows or celebrate as the case may be. The written papers presented no shocks and were on the whole balanced and fair even if a trifle long. So it was with mixed feelings that we assembled on that fateful Friday. The male nurses had traded their uniform jackets for white coats and looked clinical even if we didn't feel it. The girls had taken extra care with their uniforms, starched caps and aprons crisply shone. We stood outside the practical room, none of us daring to sit down in case we crumpled the pristine freshness of our uniforms and created a wrong first impression. Mr. Sandy came and stood with us trying to bolster our frayed nerves with little success.

Mr. Thomas was inside the practical room with the Matron. It was his task to replace the equipment that the group used on their trays and trolleys ready for the next set of combatants. We were to enter the practical room in pairs and had drawn lots for who was to go in first. Only two students were examined at a time and each session would take half-an-hour or so. The last students wouldn't be getting into the sessions until late in the afternoon and the poor girl who was to have partnered Roy would be last—and on her own. Those who were going in later in the day took off their aprons and coats and went to sit down and have a coffee. I was dying to join them but my partner and I had drawn third up and I was so nervous I would have gotten "caught short" and wanted to pee in the middle of the exam.

I'd been paired with Margaret Parker. A really attractive blonde who was just a little bit older than me. We'd worked together on several previous occasions in the 'mock practicals' and enjoyed ourselves. This time though—it was for real.

Nurses uniforms are a great 'turn on' if the rest of the assembly is all right and Margaret was assembled rather better than most. She wore a distinctive brand of heady perfume called "Intimate" that added to the lusty feelings I had towards her. I had wanted to get to know her better but as yet, the interactions of the group and the pressure of work hadn't afforded an opportunity to develop anything more than a one of the gang friendship. There would be no stirring in my loins this morning anyway—I was too bloody scared.

The first pair of students came out of the practical room smiling and had just enough time to give us the thumbs up before Mr. Sandy whisked them away. Communication between candidates was not allowed.

We stood in the corridor in a strained silence. I felt I should be looking at a textbook or something but on reflection decided that it was too late to try and absorb any new information anyway. Every minute seemed like an hour but each time that I checked my watch the hands had barely seemed to move. At last the door to the 'prac' room burst open and a tearful Helen dashed past us followed by a poker faced Derek.

The flushed, moist eyed departure of Helen, usually so well prepared and composed, sent my guts into paroxysms of activity and then we two were in the practical room. Margaret and I stood in the doorway of the room and surveyed the scene like two frightened rabbits caught in the open. The room was set out as usual with two beds with models in for bedside procedures, the long centre table groaned heavy under it's multiplicity of surgical instruments, and trolleys waiting to be set. It was all there but no longer looked friendly and familiar. Mr. Thomas, apparently unconcerned at our presence, was busy replacing instruments used by our predecessors.

In the centre of the room stood Matron.

I had once heard a charge nurse describe her as a bedworthy wench but at this moment she looked nothing like his description. She was dressed in the traditional matron's uniform of navy blue with a lace ruff round the neck and a row of medal ribbons on her rather ample chest. She was a big woman standing about five foot nine and weighing some sixteen stone. She looked slightly taller in her Victorian button up boots and with the lace nurses cap which was fastened under her chin. She was—Matron.

With a crook of her little finger she beckoned us towards her. We'd all been issued with numbers for the impersonal requirements of the examinations and we crossed the room quickly to present them to her. She made a note of them on a clipboard lying on the nearby table and gave us our first task.

Margaret and I almost ran to the bedside with relief 'change the bottom sheet with the patient lying flat in bed'—easy—we had rehearsed it so often before. All trace of nerves disappeared as we got involved with our task. We worked quickly and kept up a steady flow of conversation with our plastic patient to show we knew how to act in real life. Once the task was over we made an elaborate show of washing our hands—we even remembered that little pantomime.

The easy part of the examination over we reported back to Matron for a new assignment. Margaret was sent to prepare a trolley for a procedure and I was directed to accompany Matron to the drug cupboard. For the next ten minutes I spent an awkward time stumbling to answer her questions about the various medicines and their methods of administration. I thought I was acquitting myself well until the conversation changed to lotions and measurements.

"How many minims in a millilitre?" She asked.

I was lost, vaguely I recalled that minims were drops but conversions to that flaming French metric system had always been beyond me. I could feel myself growing redder as I searched the dim and distant reaches of my mind for an answer. Everything was blank. Mr. Sandy had given us strict instructions on how to behave if we didn't know an answer.

"First stall, then, if the answer still doesn't come say "I did know the answer but I just cannot recall it.""

This technique was based on the premise the examiner was there to find our what you know and not what you had forgotten. It was hoped they would be inclined to ask you another question. A straight out *"I don't know"* inferred a lack of knowledge and could be marked against you. I only hoped someone had explained all this to Matron.

"Well nurse?"

The usual question and statement all rolled into one. Obviously my stalling time was up. I looked at the floor trying to avoid her eyes and gain a bit more time. My gaze rested on matrons highly polished button boots and in sheer desperation I counted the number of buttons and blurted out.

"Fifteen matron."

"Congratulations—you're the only nurse to give the correct answer to that question in a long time. Please set up for a lumbar puncture." She was actually smiling at me.

If there's a trolley all mental health nurses know off by heart it's a lumbar puncture. I couldn't believe my luck. Leaving Margaret to present her trolley to Matron I moved quickly out of the firing line.

It was the longest half-hour of my life.

After presentation of the lumbar puncture trolley, the practical was over and Matron was letting us go. All the way down the corridor to the coffee lounge Margaret and I compared notes. No massive blunders, a joint task we both knew, a slice of good luck and it was all over.

Matron's Button Shoes

We were not due back in the training school until mid afternoon when we would get our results. This being the case Margaret and I went off to the village pub for lunch. It was strictly against the rules but after the trauma of the practical we felt we could risk anything. I used the time well and was able to arrange with Margaret that we have a quiet party of our own after the group celebrations were over. Room 56 in the male staff block was going to be a very pleasant place to be providing I remembered my father's advice.

By half past three the whole class was assembled in the Nurse Training School. It was just like the first day of P.T.S over again. Although we sat in small groups round the tables no one talked, we just waited. Half an hour later Mr. Thomas came out of his office and without speaking he attached a sheet of paper to the students notice board. He walked back into the office avoiding the eyes of his students and closed the door behind him. Helen, who was nearest to the board strolled over to read it. She turned, face flushed, eyes bright, laughing and crying at the same time.

"Hey everybody! It's the results, we've all passed."

There was an instant clamour as we all tried to get to the notice board at once. It was true. We'd all passed. What was more, Margaret and I had come top in the practical with ninety five percent . . . . Good old Matron.

The office door opened again to reveal smiling Messrs. Thomas and Sandy.

"Congratulations to you all." They chorused.

We rounded on them, all talking at once. Inviting them for a drink, which of course they declined. After a while order was restored. There was to be no post examination of papers and we had to report to the administration before Monday to find out our ward allocation/duties. School was over for a while and so too was the pretend. We were going to work with real people.

Chapter 4

Caring for the Kids

My first ward allocation was the children's ward. When I mentioned this to the others in the resident staff quarters they fell about laughing and made remarks like *"snottin and pottin."* I didn't take much notice. After all I'd passed out from P.T.S. and had, at least, some basic skills to contribute.

Any misconceived ideas I had about helping patients were dispelled on the first morning.

I reported to the charge nurse at seven am on the dot. Joe, Mr. Jackson to me, didn't seem pleased even though he seemed to appreciate my help when I had been allocated to his ward before I commenced in the training school.

Apparently, like many of his contemporaries, he viewed students as troublesome people who kept asking questions and I was now a student.

Joe, had fifty-six children on his ward. They slept in beds twelve inches apart in a long open dormitory. Being a children's ward it was situated on the ground floor of a three story building.

All wards in the hospital were of similar design and I knew my way round at once.

There was a communal day-room where the children who were ambulant played and were fed:

A gallery where the worker patients ate their meals and opposite which their single rooms or side-rooms were sited: *'A side-room only has a door handle on the outside so when you are put to bed and the door closed there's no way out from the inside.'*

A verandah leading to the airing court or playground:

The charge nurses office with the kitchen just opposite:

And of course the very important toilet annexe.

All of this was Mr. Jacksons kingdom and home for fifty six children.

Joe was of the same generation as most of the senior staff and his reason for entry into the service was about the same. He was in the long queue for promotion and was waiting for *"dead men's boots."* Being only five feet three, thin faced and of slight build he'd been allocated the children's ward instead of one of the adult units. I assume I'd received a similar consideration from the chiefs' office because of my age.

Joe's team consisted of a deputy charge, an occasional staff nurse, two Italian assistants who could not speak much English and myself. I wasn't sure about the Italians. They seemed to understand the pay and conditions of service O.K but whenever I asked them to do a job of work or just lend a hand, they'd look me straight in the eye and say,

"No speaka da English."

The off duty roster was organised in such a way that Joe very rarely met up with his deputy and on the few occasions when he did the chiefs' office would send the deputy out relieving on another ward. The roster gave Joe an average of four people a day on duty to care for the fifty six children and do all the domestic work necessary in a ward of that size.

The shift hours were long, thirteen hours a day, the children were all severe or profoundly retarded (intellectually disabled) with accompanying multiple handicaps making them very highly dependent. Which had the effect of reducing care to two types.

Type 1 Those children who were mobile were got up in the morning to spend their day in the day room.

Type 2 Those children who were more severely handicapped spent the whole of their lives in cots in the dormitory.

One member of staff worked the shift in the dormitory, because those patients were less active, while the remaining two worked in the day room. Joe worked in his office except for mealtimes when he'd don a white coat and serve up the food. The ward was only as good as the worker patients allowed.

Worker patients functioned as nursing assistants. They performed most of the routine duties like dressing, bathing and changing the severely handicapped children. Sweeping the floors and polishing them with the inevitable bumpers. Keeping the place tidy, running messages for the staff and helping with the feeding.

The worker patient had usually come to the institution from the magistrates or criminal courts and they laboured hard in the vain hope their good conduct would eventually lead to a discharge back to the community. It was truly a vain hope because if a good worker patient's discharge did rear its head. The charge, or one of the other staff, would provoke him into some act of violence.

Patients seldom attacked staff so it was quite a safe thing to do. The patients usually reacted to provocation by breaking windows or turning the violence in on themselves. *'Going up the pole'* as it was called could set a worker patients discharge back for a period of at least six months, which was the reason for the provocation in the first place. Most of this aggravation was beyond the limit whereby a normal person would be forced to take some action and came from the realisation that a good worker patient was often far more use to a charge nurse than two Italian assistants who *'No speaka da Inglis.'*

In addition, there was an unwritten rule among the doctors who were able to organise a discharge that they didn't take risks with people who could be aggressive.

The student nurse was very low in the pecking order on Joe's ward. I think it was because that little bit of learning frightened him. My roll revolved mainly round the dormitory with the severely disabled children in their beds. Perhaps Joe equated this with nursing the sick.

Joe's comprehension of things medical was small and his perversion of the English language beyond belief. With true rustic charm he'd reduced all the drugs prescribed for the children to 'thingys' and 'watsamacallits'. The ward was filled with 'tubercular chairs' and once after the dormitory was redecorated he confided:

"I dont mind the one with the G-nommies, but prefer the one with the hefalunts and altogether I would have preferred Murials." Traveling to the village on the bus one evening after work. I chanced to sit behind Joe and one of the other charges of the same ilk. Their conversation is still emblazoned on my heart even after the passage of time.

"Did thy go to bowls finals?" Asked Joe.
"Aye." Offered his colleague.
"Who were in't final then?"
"Oh! Watsisname."
"O-aye! Who was 'e playin'?"
"Thingymebob."
"O-yes, well who won?"
"O, tother mon won."
"O-aye."

I swear to this day that both Joe and his friend understood that conversation and could identify all the players.

Note: I leave it to the reader to work out what Joe and his colleagues were saying else find someone from Yorkshire, England. They will be able to tell you.

The first time I saw Joe walk round his charges giving the medicines out in his own inimitable way I began to doubt the value of all the time spent in the training school learning nursing procedures. His application brought a new dimension to the caring role.

Whenever he was doing anything which brought him into contact with the children Joe wore a long white coat to provide the right clinical atmosphere.

In order to do the drug round he'd fill the right hand pocket of the coat with medicine bottles from the drug cupboard. All the children were lined up round the walls of the day room, he took a bottle from his right-hand pocket and read the name out loud, popped the pill into the mouth of the appropriate child. The bottle, of the pill just given, was then placed in the left-hand pocket of his coat.

One morning, after I'd been working on the ward for a couple of weeks, I had occasion to ask Joe about one of the children in the dormitory who was spiking a temperature. I walked into the day room just as he was in the middle of his medicine round. A bottle was taken from his right hand pocket, a name called and the pill popped into an open and expectant child's mouth. The bottle was then placed into the left hand pocket. At that moment, one of the children thumped the boy next to him.

Reasons are not always necessary for violence in the world of children no more than they are in the world of adults. However, the net result of this current outbreak was to interrupt all other activity until the warring couple had been separated and peace restored. When at last order prevailed Joe continued with his medicine round. Only now there was a noticeable difference. He was taking the medicines from his left-hand pocket. Giving the pill and returning the bottle to his right. It took several minutes for the significance of this to dawn on me and by the time it did the drug round was over.

This accounted for a phenomena, which always struck me as odd from the day I started work on the ward. Some days half of the children were lethargic to the point of falling over and on other days were so hyperactive they were climbing up the curtains. Now I knew the answer. Some days they had a double dose of their drugs and on others they had none.

I asked my student colleagues who were more advanced in their training what I should do about this situation and was told.

"Change it when you're in charge."

No one could challenge the system from our humble level and for the moment Joe was in charge. To challenge the system was to be branded a troublemaker throughout the hospital and receive more than a fair share of dirty jobs. Many a good potential nurse was and still is, forced out of the service in this manner.

I worked on the children's ward for an uninterrupted nine months. Although I got to know the children very well, there was never enough time to spend with them in a teaching and learning situation. Ten fortunate children started to go to the hospital school each day for a couple of hours while the remaining forty-six just stayed on the ward. The nurse's life was an endless round of bathing, cleaning, feeding, changing, and then more bathing.

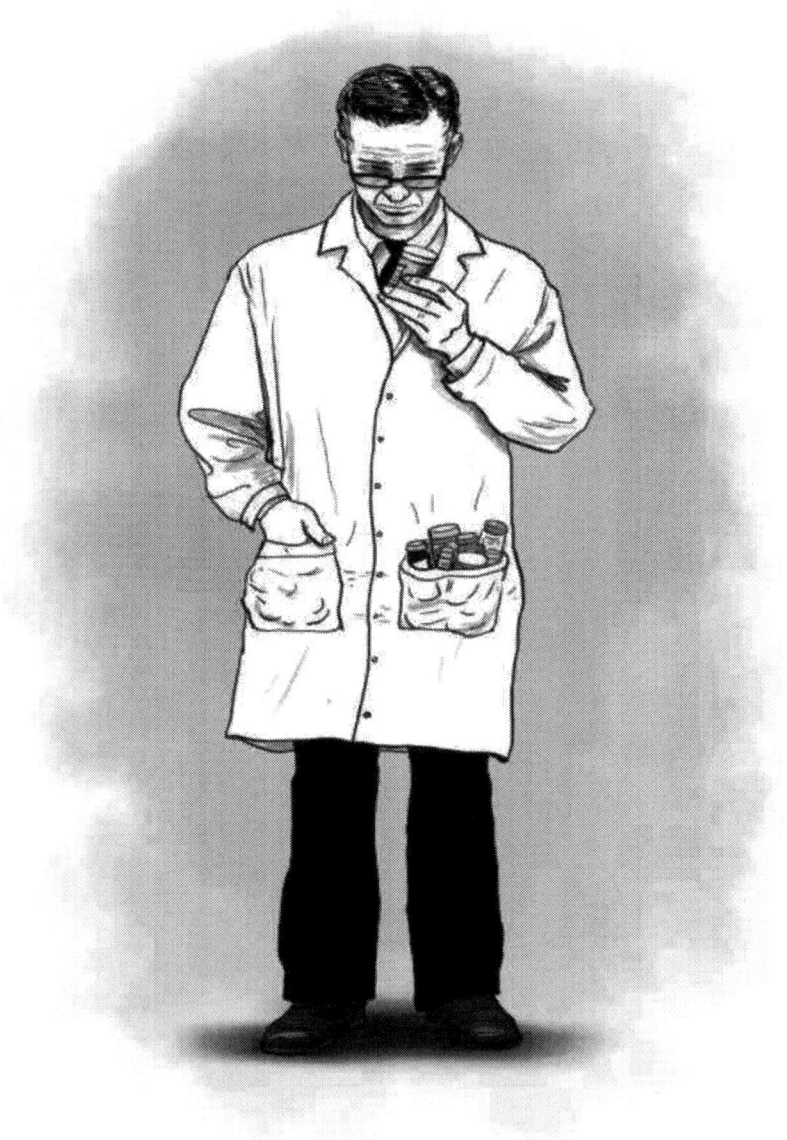

Joe doing his pill round

The children enjoyed a rich and varied diet except for a few of those frail and fragile children living in cots in the dormitory. Most had cerebral palsy with other associated conditions like hydrocephaly, or severe intellectual impairment. These children had to be fed and so their staple evening meal was "Pobs." A mixture of bread, broken up and soaked in warm milk, with a spoonful of cod liver oil and malt mixed in and a raw egg floating on the top.

I was assured it was a nourishing meal but I always seemed to get the heaves when I was feeding this mixture to a child and was grateful for the ward workers who would cheerfully take over.

Occasionally one of the students on the ward, got the chance to take the children outside into the airing-court and play with our two toys. A rocking horse and a roundabout. The toys had been put there by some long past management committee to differentiate the children's ward from the others.

Most of the time the children in the dayroom were left to their own devices whilst those in the dormitory lay in bed and looked at the ceiling. The nurses, well! we just chased our tails trying to get the routine tasks accomplished.

Enema morning

For one reason or another over a month had gone by and I hadn't been on the ward for enema morning. Enema mornings were on Tuesdays and Thursdays and I'd either been off duty, on extra duties in other wards or on lecture days in the training school. On many occasions I'd heard the other staff talk about enema morning and of course I knew how to give one and what an enema was for. But I ask you.... Enema morning.

Well this Thursday I was on duty and was going to find out.

"We'll start after breakfast." Said Joe, when I reported for duty, "dormitory first."

I was back early that morning after breakfast and stood waiting patiently for Joe in the dormitory. I was quite proud of the group of twenty patients in their cots mainly because we'd managed to keep them all free of pressure sores despite the lifetime in bed.

At the appointed time Mr. Jackson appeared at the dormitory door wearing the inevitable white coat denoting clinical procedure. It looked a bit incongruous because in one hand he was carrying an enamel bucket filled with green soapy liquid and a length of what appeared to be rubber tubing with a bulb in the middle and a nozzle in the other. In the school we'd been taught to give enemas with a funnel and tubing. Now I was to learn the ward technique using a Higginsons syringe. Behind Joe one of the worker patients wheeled a trolley full of clean linen and a bag for the soiled linen.

"We'll start down this side." said Joe with a nod of his head. "And come back down t'other."

He moved towards the beds on the right side of the dormitory. No one thought it necessary to screen the beds as Joe set to his appointed task with gusto. The cot sides were dropped and the child in the first bed was rolled onto his left side. Joe pulled a piece of cotton wool out of his jacket pocket and a tube of KY Jelly from the other. Quickly he lubricated one end of the Higginsons syringe and inserted this into the child's rectum. A small bowl was produced by the worker patient and a pint of fluid from the bucket was placed on the bed.

Using the Higginsons syringe Joe pumped the pint of green soapy slime into the child's lower bowels. Replacing the covers, he lifted up the cot sides and moved swiftly to the next bed where the procedure was repeated.

He continued until an enema was administered to every child in the dormitory.

The children were left to evacuate their bowels in the beds as Joe went off to distribute the doubtful benefits of enema to the ambulant children. One of the worker patients with the trolley of clean linen was left behind with me to help change the beds.

After about twenty minutes the dormitory began to smell like a stable even with all the windows open. The worker patient, who was experienced in these matters, judged that the enemas had been effective.

"Right," he said, "lets get started."

He filled a bowl with warm soapy washing water, collected some clean linen from the trolley and moved towards the first bed. He called for two, less senior ward workers to come and handle the soiled bedding. About an hour later we'd cleaned and changed every patient—but the smell, that seemed to remain, for ever.

In some ways the hospital was reaping what it had sown. The unrestricted use of enema's on these children robbed them of their natural bowel actions. Consequently the use of the enema had become an integral part of the children's care.

A week later I was able to see the enema's given to the ambulant children. The treatment was given in a similar manner to the dormitory but with the children lying on a rubber mackintosh and towel on the floor of the ablutions block. All round the room were small children's training pots and toilets. One by one the children were led in, given their enema and seated on the pot. Another student visiting the ward called into the ablutions to see where all the staff were. He walked into the room and sniffed long and loud.

"Ahh!" he said, "smell that therapeutic environment."

For all the chaos that reigned on the children's ward and even though there was little or no educational or therapeutic stimulation for them. Physically the children were fit and well. All the time I worked in the hospital I never saw an undernourished child or a bed sore in the bed-ridden group.

Nor—was any one of them constipated.

Chapter 5

The Hospital Dance

Life for most residents was filled with activity. Many of the worker/patients worked on the wards or in the power station where the hospital generated its own power (*DC only*). Some were employed in the kitchens, laundry, gardens and of course the farm.

Much sought after jobs were in the maintenance department where trades were conducted and the skills learned could often lead to employment when discharged to the community. Best of all the maintenance staff had opportunities to work in the female side of the hospital.

The wards, in addition to television, contained pool tables and opportunities for hobbies and interest. While discussion and remedial education groups were to be found in most day rooms. Occasionally one of the staff would crank up the ward piano and interest a group in a sing-along with popular tunes.

Most importantly, in the winter months, we held the hospital dances. These were part of the patients recreational activities and were held in the much lauded ballroom featured in the hospitals publicity brochure.

The ballroom was common ground, being situated between the male and female administration blocks. Entrances led into the hall from both the male side of the hospitals administration wing and via a similar route from the female side. The ward workers and more able residents looked forward to this evening with an enthusiasm bordering on hysteria. All day they'd talk of nothing else except they were going to meet their woman at the dance.

By five o clock all work on the ward ceased. Children had suffered hasty meals thrust into reluctant mouths and the workers disappeared to get ready. The dances always started promptly at six p.m. so they could end by seven forty five p.m. This allowed the nurses to return the patients to ward and still be able to go off duty at the appointed time of eight o clock.

Best clothing was extracted from all manner of places. Those privileged few who had rooms of their own seemed to have no problems. Trousers pressed under mattresses were brought into view and shirts which were better than the usual hospital issue suddenly appeared from under pillow cases. Patients who lived in dormitories had to rely on the generosity of the charge nurse to outfit them from the communal stock room.

This system added to the charges power as patients who were the most willing workers always got outfitted first.

Once patients were dressed the presents started to come out. In an institution where the individual had no wardrobes or bedside lockers, the patients still managed to find private places to store some precious prizes. An apple saved from a fruit ration, a necklace made from silver toffee and cigarette paper, a few sweets saved from token shopping or a parcel from home. These were not always saved for the women out of love but were offered to the girlfriend only if there was a gift in exchange.

Intricate necklace made of sweet wrappers and silver paper

The patients were collected for the dance by nursing staff rostered for that duty. The list of extra tasks outside of ward duties was posted outside the chief's office the evening before to indicate who the fortunate staff were. It was not considered a privilege to be sent to the dance even though the staff got off the ward for a short time.

My term on the children's ward was nearing its end as I was rostered for dance duty. Joe was, as usual, about as helpful as the body at a funeral, present but not actually doing anything.

"Report to the subs office they'll tell 'e what to do." Then he dismissed me with a wave of his hand.

Alf gave me a piece of paper with five ward names written neatly on the left hand margin.

"Collect the patients from those five wards lad and write the numbers in by each ward." He smiled as if enjoying some private joke.

"Oh! And don't lose any of the buggers on the way . . . . Enjoy th'self."

I set off on my round. It was getting dark and the lights were on along the covered walkway to the wards. I opened the first door on the list of wards with my pass key.

"Dance." I yelled at the top of my voice, imitating the procedure I'd witnessed from inside the ward on previous occasions.

"Fifteen mister." Came the reply from the bright lights inside the ward. I counted fifteen patients out onto the main corridor and made a note of the number on my piece of paper. The patients were used to the procedure and lined up in two's slightly ahead of me. The corridor was now filling up with staff on 'point duty'. They were deployed along the corridors to ensure none of the patients absconded or wandered off whilst the escorting staff were occupied opening ward doors and counting. All of them were in full uniform, rugged up against standing around on a cold winter evening.

At the same time they were aware *"Bill the Bastard"* was on duty so no one was taking any chances. I continued on my way, marching my charges in front of me and halting at each ward I was due to collect from. Once at the main hall door we were greeted by one of the Assistant Chiefs with a large book. He barely glanced at me. The uniform cap was sufficient to tell him which one of the group was staff.

"Number Mister?." It was the inevitable question.

"Forty five sir." I answered handing him my list. We stood patiently while he copied my figures into his book.

"Right Mister," said the chief, handing me back my piece of paper ready for the return journey, "in you go."

I marched my expectant Romeo's into the hall.

The hospital band was already in place. There were only three of them, all nursing staff. They were paid ten pounds a year extra for being in the band. At one time there had been over twenty staff in the orchestra but the number had been allowed to dwindle over the years. All the hospital had left was a double bass, piano and drums.

As usual, and by design, the males arrived before the females. My group took their places in the seats suitably arranged along one side of the hall. I joined the staff already standing slightly in front of the row of seats occupied by the patients. We formed a human barrier between them and the seats yet to be occupied by the females. When all the male patients were in place an expectant hush fell over the hall.

Suddenly the rear doors leading to the female corridor were unlocked and flung open. The female patients were led in preceded by one of the Assistant Matrons. The ladies moved efficiently into place along the opposite side of the hall, some of them jockeying for positions facing their boy friends. That is, if once a month contact on a dance floor and the rest of the time dreaming can be called a boy friend / girl friend relationship. The female staff formed the same human barrier as their male counterparts. Neither group was allowed to pass *"no-mans-land"* in the middle of the hall until the first chord was struck.

Before the dance could get underway the sub officer and Assistant Matron conferred on numbers. As a result the chief approached one of the male staff nearest the door of the hall.

"Not enough females Mister" he said to male nurse." Take five of yours back to the ward."

Five crestfallen individuals were chosen and exited with the nurse. The dance was over for them before it had begun.

One of the girls called out to the boys. At least she got the first syllable out before the rest of her sentence was frozen into silence on her lips by the frosty look she received from the Assistant Matron.

The sub officer walked along the row of male staff and then moving slightly towards the centre of the room beckoned two male nurses towards him. This part of the ritual of the dance left the two staff members standing one at either end of the dance floor. The Assistant Matron repeated the exercise with two of her staff and they went and stood next to the males. Their job was to act as end posts and ensure the patients danced round them, and the room in a clockwise direction.

I offered up a silent prayer of thanks that I'd not been asked to undertake this job on my first dance. A slight nod from the chief and the dance was underway.

As the first chord was struck both male and female patients leapt from their seats like all the hounds of hell were after them. They converged on the middle of the hall as though it was a race to get to the middle first. Total chaos reigned for a few seconds as each sought out their respective partners. Having found one another, parcels and presents were swapped in a frenzy of activity and after a quick inspection stuffed in pockets or down the front of dresses. As order was restored the couples moved off in the regulation clockwise direction.

Most patients could not dance so just clasped their partner firmly and marched, sometimes the male leading, sometimes the female and on occasions crab-like, round the end-post staff.

Come Dancing

I joined the rest of my colleagues. Our task was to patrol the floor looking for patients snogging or worse and send them off the dance floor to their respective sides of the room. Starved of love and tactile contact the patients made the most of having someone warm to cuddle up to. Occasionally baser instincts took over and it wasn't uncommon for a young man to be sent back to the side of the ballroom for trying to have sex with his partner during the slow waltz.

Sex in this context was usually restricted to copping a quick feel at some forbidden part of the others anatomy. The first offense was to miss the next dance the second was back to the ward.

Another, unwritten rule was; Patients were not allowed to have three consecutive dances with the same partner; and many a disappointed couple was sent off the floor for this breach of the rules

Like many of the hospital functions it was an "us and them" situation and I couldn't help but reflect on its farcical nature.

It was only a few months earlier I'd left Manchester where Jimmy Saville was holding lunch time dance sessions at the Plaza Ballroom.

Smooch time, as it was known, was quite an acceptable part of the modern dance scene. With dim lights, slow soft music and copious amounts of touchy-feely in the massed middle of the dance floor.

Not however, in the world of Mental Health, it could perhaps make you blind.

Televisions 'Come Dancing' was never like this. It was a case of grab your lady tightly and walk, vaguely in time to the music in a clockwise direction round the floor. While all the time the band thumped out its regular. Bum, tit, tit rhythm

For most of the patients it didn't matter what the tune or dance was, their progress round the floor remained the same. As soon as the music ended the couples split up and went to their respective sides of the hall like boxers separating at the sound of the bell.

The only communication between male and female nurses was the odd raising of eyebrows in recognition. It was just 'not done' to speak to one another except at senior officer level in case we gave the patients ideas. Margaret was there with some of the female patients and although we had a date in the staff club later, I had to content myself with a slight nod in her direction. Even this show of familiarity earned me a severe look from the Assistant Matron. Another of my hopes dashed. I must have been very naive because I'd actually thought I was going dancing.

All too soon for the patients the ball was over and they lined up ready for 'home'. As was to be expected the males had to wait patiently while the females left the hall.

It was now time to collect my patients and check that I was going back with the same number of bodies I arrived with. One of the males risked being banned from the next dance by rushing across the room with a last minute message for his girl. That would earn his escorting staff a severe warning from the chief about discipline and control.

The return to the wards was uneventful. Point duty staff were in their places and as I opened each ward door the patients trooped in allowing me to count them and call the number to the staff waiting inside the door.

On one occasion when the dance had gone on later than usual due to the band leaders watch stopping. The staff were all in a hurry to get home. Nurses rushed their patients along the corridors. Ward doors were flung open with much banging and crashing—numbers were called up the corridors—and bodies pushed inside each doorway. This resulted in several patients being placed in the wrong ward for the night however, they were all re-slotted into the right beds the next day and dances were never allowed to run late—ever again.

Chapter 6

On Violence

Of course violence existed. Most of the staff had started work at the hospital long before any of the modern therapeutic drugs came into being. They'd been brought up with the legend that force and a hard fist was the only way to control the violent patient. Many subtle forms of violence existed as well as direct physical assault.

One of the most frightening of these was the use of the side-room. These had grown from the padded cell that had a period of success in the 1930's. Ostensibly in Halley Hospital the side room was made into a bedroom for the mild and moderately intellectually disabled person. They were infinitely preferable to sleeping in a dormitory with fifty or sixty others. The room, although seen as a status symbol by many of the patients had one considerable disadvantage. There was only a door handle on the outside. Once you were in the room for the night, there you stayed if the staff so chose. In addition the light switch to the room was on the outside of the door so the patient had no control over his illumination. Lights out was a time determined by staff.

The side room had no window and therefore always received its illumination from the single bulb placed high up in the ceiling. Only very trusted patients were allowed to sleep with their door open. A small, reinforced glass spy hole in the door bore grim testament to the rooms former use.

In some wards the side rooms had a dual purpose. Some were indeed used as bedrooms for the more able and co-operative patients while others were reserved for a much more sinister purpose. They were used as a means of behaviour control. A place where an aggressive or disruptive patient could be locked in for days with no contact with others save for the small amount of food issued at mealtimes. Often the threat of the side room was all that was needed to control inappropriate behaviours.

The most dangerous part of the side-room control system was that it was rather arbitrarily administered on the whim of the nurse in charge of the ward at the time. Even today the use of seclusion is part of the behaviour control strategy of most large and small institutions. In prisons it is called solitary confinement and in institutions for the mentally retarded it is called 'time out'. In aged care facilities the person has their call bell taken away or if they are really disruptive they can score themselves a private room.—Rewarded for behaving badly.

Theoretically time out is strictly controlled and monitored but like most systems is still open to abuse.

The side rooms at Halley Hospital dehumanized the patients and seemed to detract from the staff ability to see their charges as real people. The more aggressive residents became, they were, in the attitude of some of the staff, a form of sub-human species who's presence interfered with the smooth running of the institution. They had to be brought under control at all costs. There was a barrier between the staff and patients that could never be passed. We were staff. Never to be questioned in our God-like authority. They were patients, there to obey.

Physical violence was not uncommon both from staff and patients. The staff were less violent than the patients, they didn't need to use much force as they held all the trump cards. Meals, Dances, Cigarettes and pocket money and even visits, the staff controlled the currency of the institution.

Anyway, anyone who had a violent nature could, as a last resort, be sent to a refractory (punishment) ward and lose what precious freedoms still remained to him. Most patients were only driven to violence when all forces seemed against him and reason was lost in a desperate kick against the system. A few however, were by their very nature, violent and this was the reason for their hospitalization.

The first time I met up with mindless violence from a patient was nearly my last. I was standing on the verandah of the children's ward talking to David, one of the worker patients and watching the children enjoy a brief moment of sunshine.

I was leaning on the railings discussing with David aspirations about his future. Like many he was looking for a discharge back to a community, which had rejected him. As I turned my head towards him It was just in time to see a clenched fist about two inches from my face. In that kind of situation there is no where to go. Everything went black and I felt myself falling. I wasn't knocked out because I remember bringing my legs up to protect my stomach and covering my face with my arms in anticipation of the boot which must surely follow.

Instead, through my punchy haze I heard a yell and then a thud. One of my colleagues, one of the Italians, was walking along the gallery and witnessed David's attack.

Calling for assistance he ran out onto the verandah and, in order to protect both himself and me he clouted David over the head with a chair. At the inquiry which followed David was asked why he'd hit me. His reply was a revelation:-

"I was having a rotten day and didn't feel very well. The charge had been getting on to me and no one wanted to listen. I felt this urge to hit out and you were the nearest.—No hard feelings."

David offered his hand in apology. It was equally obvious he had no hard feelings against the member of staff who'd hit him either. The incident made me realise the lack of skill and knowledge I had in dealing with people like David. If I'd been more experienced I may have noticed the subtle warning signs and been alerted to his agitation. Instead, I became a victim of a system which required a young inexperienced person to deal as best he can with such a vast and complex problem.

Physical punishment, in opposition to violence, is always a source of heated debate in most societies let alone institutions. Especially when it comes to controlling inappropriate behaviour in children by giving them a smack. In most western cultures, hospitals and services for children have outlawed the practice of giving a short sharp slap for disruptive behaviour. Yet the people responsible for controlling behaviours, the doctors and occasionally psychologists, have no hesitation in calling for an increase in a sedation medication used to quieten violent and aggressive children.

I have to ask the question, which is the more violent? Giving someone a slap on the back of the hands or legs, giving them a label and sticking a needle in them zapping them out for the day, or even the use of mind bending drugs for years and years and years without any real evidence about the long term effects.

Assault with an instrument of corporal punishment is, in my book, stupid because the cane, strap or whatever other implement has no feeling and injury can be the result. However, a slap with the open hand can hurt the administrator as well as the recipient. So, hopefully they will stop when it hurts.

In Halley Hospital, staff violence was infrequent, but existed. There were several types of violent staff. Firstly there was the violence brought about by the intolerable working conditions. I have mentioned we didn't have many staff on the children's ward. With a working day of thirteen hours it was possible, as I know to my cost when I argued with Joe, to spend the whole of the working day, with the exception of meal breaks, bathing incontinent children.

On days when we had less than four staff on duty it meant. Joe in the office all day, one staff in the dormitory and one staff in the playroom with over thirty noisy, incontinent and disturbed children. Parents could not manage the behaviour at home on a one to one basis and in our wisdom we were attempting to care and manage their inappropriate behaviour in a large group.

The day room would reek of excreta. A mop and bucket stood in the corner. Filled with disinfectant it was called into regular use to mop up the puddles of urine, which constantly stained the wooden floor. If it was a cold winter day the windows were firmly closed against the elements and as the hours passed the mixed odours of urine, faeces and disinfectant got stronger. After a while staff became impervious to the smell and it only hit them when they returned to the ward from a meal break.

Sadly there were no toys for the children to play with and the only diversion was the noise of a transistor radio, if one of the staff remembered to bring one to work. On special days one of the staff would attempt to thump out a tune on the battered old piano in the corner of the room. Our employer, the Health Service seemingly wouldn't send it's maintenance staff out to dig a hole without a shovel but it expected the nurses to look after disturbed children without toys or basic educational equipment.

In the corner of the day room, one would frequently find a very disturbed child. He was looking out at the world through hollow, almost haunted eyes. No one seemed to know what was going on behind those eyes, but, it could only have been painful. All day long a drawn out moan would emit from the suffering youngster. Any parent who has coped with children teething and survived the attendant whining will know how much a constant whine can get on the nerves.

To stay in the day room with such a noise, coupled with the pools of pee and bottoms to wipe, with fighting and destructive children to separate, with a burning need to make some progress of a positive nature with at least one child. A thirteen hour day can seem like a life sentence.

Thus, by five-o clock in the evening a well placed kick or tap will alter the tone of the whine if nothing else. The treatment of awkward children in this manner has an escalatory effect. Being hit by one of the staff was better than being ignored.

With so many children for one person to look after, then those who's behaviour was acceptable were often the ones ignored. The child sees the "naughty boy" receive staff attention, albeit of a negative nature, and therefore misbehaves himself to get his own share.

Unfortunately this form of violence was all too common in the early days at Halley hospital, precipitated by the frustration of not having enough pairs of hands. Of course, such a situation could not occur today? Could it?

Another form of staff violence was that used in the protection of themselves from aggressive patients. There were occasions when the sedation meted out to the patients didn't quite reach the levels required to control their violent proclivities. Then seemingly unprovoked attacks on staff occurred. Most of the time these violent patients could be talked through their aggressive stage if the staff were skilled and experienced. However, there are those who wouldn't be reasoned with.

On such occasions a counter act of aggression was required from the nurses to protect themselves. The danger in those situations occurred when the aggression from the nurse reached the stage of undue force as fear and frustration welled up together. It wasn't uncommon to see a restraining arm, twisted up the patients back, being given an extra jerk making the patient call out in pain.

The staff were always expected to be in control of the situation and their retaliation to violence cannot be condoned but at least it can be understood.

I felt the same sense of frustration as my colleagues. I feared some of the more violent patients just as much as the next member of staff. All the platitudes in the world, given by the hospital administrators, doctors and psychologists who weren't involved with the patients on a day to day basis, didn't make the nursing task any easier or make the fear go away.

In fact the war of words only highlighted some of the rifts between, the administration, who couldn't understand the need for all this equipment, the doctors, psychologists, and experts who recommend treatments and programmes which couldn't be carried out because of the manpower shortage, and the nurses who were on the front of the battlefield and always being told they were doing it wrong.

The final form of violence was not acceptable to anyone. The nature of the hospital as a totally self contained institution not only attracted those who care, but a fringe group from society who have social and emotional problems of their own. The mentally handicapped and psychiatric hospital, being a therapeutic community, provided these people with a place in which to work out their personal problems.

Stan was one of these people. One morning I was working in the children's ward dormitory, making beds. Joe was in his office (he was always in the office). One of the assistant nurses was bathing patients and the other, Stan, was in the day room.

Billy, one of our incontinent and hyperactive children could be heard throughout the ward. "Booooo, zum, zum, zum,"

His nonsense noises would go on for hours when he was happy, usually delivered at the top of his voice. On this occasion they only lasted for about ten minutes then there was an abrupt silence. It took a second or two for the silence to register. I hurried up to the dayroom to see if there was a problem. There wasn't. Billy was fast asleep in a chair. It was unusual for him to sleep so early in the day, but, I assumed that Joe had done one of his spectacular medicine rounds.

"Everything alright." I asked of Stan.

"Sure." He replied.

I spent a couple of minutes exchanging pleasantries and then I went back to work in my dormitory. Later on, over a meal break, I mentioned Billy sleeping to one of my student pals. It was nothing-specific just idle conversation but his reply startled me. He mentioned that he expected Stan was on duty in the day room.

"How do you know it was him?" I asked, curiosity aroused.

"Easy," he said, "I've worked with him before. If there's a noisy patient getting on his nerves, and, providing the patient is smaller than himself and cannot talk sense. He puts a sleeper on them."

I must have looked blank because he continued.

"It's a sort of wrestling hold round the throat. You keep it on and let go just before the patient becomes unconscious. That way they appear to be asleep. If you keep it on too long they go under."

I found the whole thing hard to believe and when I got back to the ward mentioned what I'd been told to Joe. He just dismissed the whole thing as gossip.

"Not worth bothering with," he said.

Nevertheless, it disturbed me to think it might be true and I resolved to keep a look out. Two weeks later a similar situation occurred only this time the child was not Billy but a young lad with a similar problem of making noise. As soon as the noise stopped I ran along the gallery to the day room to see what was happening. I arrived just in time to see Stan releasing his hold on the child's throat.

The attack had been made with the crook of his arm so there would be no tell tale finger marks. The child was silent and with his eyes closed looked for all the world as though he was sleeping.

"What the hell do you think your doing?" My voice rose to an embarrassing high-pitched squeak as I wrestled with the rage that was boiling inside me.

"Cutting off his gas to get some peace." Was Stan's nonchalant answer. He was about fifteen years older than me and gave me a look which said I was an interfering young fool.

"If your thinking of reporting this, forget it." He said.

"It's only your word against mine and I'll say I had him on my knee and he fell asleep."

According to the hospital hierarchical system I was more senior than this bloke on account of my bit of training. However, I had never been called on to reprimand someone in my entire life and to have a go at this guy was a test that I baulked at. Instead I decided that bigger guns than mine were needed and so I stormed out of the day room down to Joes' office. Not bothering to knock I flung open his door and in an angry breathless state of agitation related what I had just seen. To my surprise Joe didn't even move from his seat to examine the boy.

"You'll be making a lot of trouble for yourself lad and you may not get the chance to finish your training." He said.

"There's no point in crusading. You'll never stop it. The kids can't say anything d'ya'see."

"No I don't see." I yelled at him now agitated beyond reason and close to tears.

I stormed from the ward over to the Nursing Officers office.

I'd a special relationship with most of them and was sure they'd do something—but they didn't. Oh, they calmed me down and promised to look in to the incident. But nothing happened. As Alf said to me some time later, in one of his quieter and more reflective moods

"That's one of the problems. The patients cannot speak up for themselves. Conditions of work for the staff are hard. Not so much physical but the mental strain is always there. We have a high turnover of staff and a few rotten eggs will always get in. To get the proof to get them out could leave your staff afraid to touch a patient even when he is going wild with the bread knife in case someone cries 'undue force' It's the tip of an iceberg and we're afraid it will melt."

In any event, Alf moved Stan off the children's ward. Nothing was said. But he was moved off on the next staff rotation. Over the years I learned that Alf was right. The violence is the tip of an iceberg, which if it ever melts, the water level will rise so high it will probably drown all the innocents along with the few guilty ones.

Yes, violence existed then and it probably still does. I am reminded that many nursing homes and hostels are similar institutions albeit slightly smaller than Halley.

Chapter 7

The Cinema

One of the other major activities to take place in the hall was the cinema. This required the maintenance department to winch a full size cinema screen into place on the stage, change the seating from the sides of the dance floor to face the cinema screen in neat rows with a centre aisle and "hey presto"—Multiplex Cinema's who needs you.

Cinema was held on three consecutive nights once a month. The first night was for staff and their families. This was particularly useful for those members of staff who were living in the hospital staff quarters or for those who lived nearby on the hospital housing estate.

The second night for those patients who had higher abilities.

And the last night for the 'duds'. (the severely intellectual and physically disabled patients) It gave them their one night out away from the wards.

The operation of getting the patients into the hall was carried out in the same manner used for dances. The same rules as the dance also applied for the seating of people. Male patients sat on the right hand seats and the females on the left. The staff observers formed the usual human barrier between the sexes by occupying the seats along either side of the centre aisle.

There was to be no crossing over or fraternizing. Not even the passing of presents or the throwing of sweets. This didn't stop the more determined of our patients. On one occasion when I was detailed to cinema duty I felt something move under my seat. I looked down just in time to see one of our best ward workers returning from across the aisle on his hands and knees. I don't know who was more embarrassed him or me. In the event I concentrated hard on the film and when I looked again he was back in his seat.

As usual the staff weren't allowed to converse with their colleagues of the opposite sex. We had to continue observance of the regulation distancing required by the system. The assistant chief and assistant matron sat at the back of the hall and kept watch over us *'just in case'*.

The projectionist was one of the maintenance engineers who was paid extra to show the films in the evenings. He was also an avid tippler and used the solitude of the projection booth to indulge to his heart's content. The booth was well equipped with twin synchronized projectors which allowed the film to run without a break.

On *"staff nights"* the projectionist remained sober and kept the film showing without a hitch. Watching the same film three times on three consecutive nights must have bored him to tears. So, by the time the cinema outing came round for the more severely handicapped patients he was often too drunk to co-ordinate both projectors and we had to settle for frequent reel changes. At these times, or any other unscheduled break in the screening, all the house lights would be put on. The staff were required to stand up and check that each seat in their row was occupied with a body.

Occasionally, during these intervals, one of the patients would request the toilet and other staff would keep an eye on my charges while I escorted the 'requestee'. The first time I was taking some of my 'lads' to the toilet, a charge nurse called me to one side.

"Don't go yourself Mister." He said. "Just stand and keep an eye on them."

I didn't ask why as I knew that the reason for this pearl of wisdom would soon be forthcoming.

"They'll wait 'till you get your old man out and are having a pee then they'll zip up and bugger off to their seats. You'll get into trouble with the chief for not supervising and they get a laugh at your expense."

Is it any wonder that in this type of climate some of the staff began to see themselves as nothing more than prison officers and certainly not nurses. In any event, I lacked the courage to go to the loo when escorting patients, and, of course, spent some very uncomfortable evenings—with my legs crossed.

One could always tell which of the cinema days it was if you were selected to clean the hall with a working party the next morning. After the staff there was very little cleaning. After the brighter patients there were the inevitable toffee papers. After the 'duds' were little pools of pee.

The films were carefully chosen 'U' category which avoided contentious issues. No violence and definitely *'No overt Sex.'* If the film was a long one the interest of the tipsy projectionist would wane even further and the intervals between reels would get longer and longer. On the third night the whole saga seemed to take forever. On more than one occasion the reels of film got mixed up and were shown out of order. No one complained or even seemed to notice. Though 'Show Boat' will never seem to same to me after watching it split into five separate reels—shown at random.

Chapter 8

More Training

Life on the wards was interspersed with periods in the nurse training school. This was for study days or for a week or more, called blocks.

The rationale behind the system was, that as we gained more experience on the wards our theoretical knowledge should be increased.

The problem was that many of the tasks on the wards bore no relationship to the theoretical aspects of residential care for the disabled person. To compound the problem students were often given strange information by well meaning charge nurses, in an effort to explain this disparity.

"Ah! (Funny how most pieces of advice started with ah!), That may be all right over in the school but the patients aren't really like that and it won't work in the ward."

This comment was used to explain any situation which could have been changed to better the patients lot. Joe used it to explain why clinical nursing procedures wouldn't work; why behaviour modification wouldn't work; why training of any sort wouldn't work; and why recreation wasn't needed.

I was very rarely called on to put my hard won theory into practice as an unqualified member of staff, that is a student. Sometimes the fault wasn't with the charge nurses attitude either. It was purely a lack of facilities.

My first attempt at giving an injection came when one of the children started with the condition known as Status Epilepticus. That is: he was having seizures one after the other with little or no break between attacks. Such episodes are usually extremely exhausting for the patient and if untreated can result in death. Imagine if you will, running a mile flat out and then being compelled to run another immediately afterwards—and then another, and another and so on until the bodily systems can no longer function.

The treatment of choice in Halley Hospital was, following an initial enema, an injection of a drug called paraldehyde. The administrative routine was such that the drug was automatically written up on all epileptic patients case notes, "*to be given as necessary.*" This saved the doctor having to turn out and examine the patient. All that was required was the nurse call the doctor to inform him what was happening and the order to give the injection could be given over the telephone.

Joe took a delight in delegating, what he called real nursing, to the students. This was in direct contrast to many other wards where anything that vaguely resembled nursing was kept well away from the students on the grounds that, "*They're all bloody ideas and no sense.*" On this occasion Joe delegated the task of giving the injection to me.

As we were not an infirmary ward there was no clinical area in which to prepare procedures, so we used the kitchen. Small clinical items which the ward may be required to use were kept in the charges office or in the cupboard under the sink.

I found a glass syringe and stainless steel needles in a box in the office cupboard along with shaving soap and razors, button boxes, sewing materials and the tea bags for the charges 'cuppa.' The ampule of paradehyde and some spirit was located in the medicine cupboard.

It took several minutes to find the cotton wool swabs to prep the skin with. They were hiding in a jam jar under the sink in the kitchen along with the soap powder and wire wool.

The ward didn't possess any sterilizing equipment and so I boiled the syringe and needles in a pan on the kitchen stove. There was no fancy stainless steel kidney dish to put the injection requirements in to take to the bedside.

As Joe said.

"T'aint the training school here boy."

I eventually arrived at the bed side with a tea tray containing all my requirements. I had a saucer of meths dampened swabs, a pan of hot water housing a syringe and needles and the ampule of paraldehyde in my pocket. I felt, and looked, more like a waitress serving tea in a cafe than a nurse about to save a life.

Because of the disparity between the wards and the training school there was a tension between the two areas. Students were caught in the cross fire. We wanted to be good nurses and so felt a loyalty to the school and the tutors who were trying to instill in us good professional practices. On the wards however, one was often compelled by the subtle, and not so subtle, pressures of workmates to throw the book away and conform to the mediocre standard that was the norm. Ask anyone who is working in a mental health institution or Aged Care Facility.

When our group reported back to the training school for the long block of three weeks which would culminate with our first professional examinations many changes had taken place. The group had changed quite significantly.

Four of the gang from the P.T.S. had resigned and left the hospital. Two of the girls had left to get married, one by accident of pregnancy and one by design, one had left to undertake general nursing and one of the male nurses had left the service to become a lorry driver. He had a wife and two small children to support and couldn't continue on the wages he received.

Another six of the group had given up the idea of gaining professional training and opted for ward assistant status. So now we were nine, and after only one year.

I was pleased to see that Margaret was still in the group. We'd stopped going out regularly together, it was getting too serious, but it was nice to see her friendly face anyway.

The biggest change was in the tutorial staff. Mr. Thomas had left the hospital to take up an appointment in London. Although the grapevine of the staff block had warned us to expect some changes in the school none of us knew what to expect from the new principal tutor.

Some of the changes were apparent from the moment we entered the school. A library was being built, some of the classrooms had been restructured and an atmosphere of relaxed informality prevailed.

The new tutor, John Davis, introduced himself to us during the first session of the morning. He was totally different from Mr. Thomas in every respect. He was a big man dressed in a lounge suit and having none of the pseudo military air of the rest of the institution. Informal, informed and reasonable.

We now had a new set of values to assimilate instead of rules and regulations. Common sense seemed to be the order of the day with informal lectures, discussion groups and the great heresy of no uniform unless practical sessions were on the timetable. At last we were being given the chance to be people and contribute some of our ideas to the caring task. I couldn't help but think of Roy and wonder, how he'd have fared in this group.

Our days in the school became something to look forward to. Even Mr. Sandy was able to relax and be himself under the careful guidance of 'Big John'. We even found he was a sensitive and thoughtful lecturer once he got out of the dictation habit.

The new principal tutor was not only a formidable force in the nurse training school but was having some small impact on the wards.

He encouraged the charge nurses to be involved in the training of the student nurse. This gave them status and they hesitantly agreed. Slowly, although we didn't know it at the time, the hospital was beginning to lurch forward into a progressive new era. Change wasn't going to happen over night.

Working in the new, informal school, we studied harder but with much more enthusiasm and eventually the nine of us took our first professional examinations. The 'prelims' were like the end of P.T.S. exams at a more advanced level. Lady luck stayed with me and I found myself working with Margaret through a practical examination

The preparation for this test was more nerve racking than the first because the examination was taken outside our own institution at the nearby city's general hospital. Halley gave us the day off to take the practical but most of it was wasted in nervous anticipation as Margaret and I didn't get into the prac. room until late afternoon.

Our romantic flame flared for the evening in a burst of unbridled passion after the ordeal—it was not to last—just a relief from stress.

The results took six weeks in arriving, outside examinations required outside examiners. We all passed.

The grateful government rewarded us with a five shilling a week pay rise and a forty pound bonus for staying with our training thus far.

None of this mattered much compared with the change within the campus. No longer strangers to the hospital our names moved up in seniority on the off duty rosters. We were second year students—part trained.

Chapter 9

Living In

The student nurse population of the hospital was compact and distinct force with a camaraderie all of it own. Much of this close fellow-feeling stemmed from the school of nursing where we spent long hours in one another's company. This coupled with the fact that most of us were resident in the hospital cemented a special bond between us. Much as national service brought about many strange friendships, so too did living in the institution. The male staff block was situated above the male administration offices and the staff dining room. The whole of the first and second floor of the building was given to providing staff residences for the male nurses, with some thirty rooms on each floor.

Each room was rather like a cell off a long corridor. Some rooms were slightly larger than others which led to a mad scramble to approach the chiefs office for a transfer every time one of the occupants of a larger room moved out.

Before I started work at the hospital I shared a bed-room with my brother, so the luxury of a room of my own was a novelty and I think I would have lived in a cupboard if necessary during those early years. At both ends of each floor was an *'ablutions area'* consisting of two bathrooms and five wash basins. Because we had to be on duty for seven in the morning there was a mad charge from about six thirty onwards to occupy a sink or bath before going on duty.

After work the students met in the communal common room on the first floor. It was here that plans were made for the evening. Sometimes to watch T.V., sometimes to adjourn to the staff club in the grounds, sometimes to try the village pubs or even further afield in one of the nearby towns. In the early days the majority of the students tended to stick together with the group they were in school with but as size of the groups diminished in the training school so the relationships with other staff living in developed.

The people in the neighbouring rooms were an important part of the students sub-culture. No one wanted to move into a larger room if it meant moving too far away from the student group or placed you next door to one of the more senior resident staff. I was fortunate enough to have two of my closest friends living next door to me.

On one side of "*room 56,*" lived Frank. He was a post graduate student nurse having completed some training in a large mental hospital and had years of experience at 'living-in.'

Frank adopted many strategies to cope with the frustrations of living on top of the job and working long hours. One of these was to make his room as comfortable as possible including the introduction of forbidden things like his pet budgie. His best effort was a 'live-in' girl friend.

The Night Superintendents office was situated at the bottom of the stairs leading to the resident staff quarters so getting a girl up to your room required stealth and some nerve. He was not a creature of habit and undertook his rounds on an irregular basis. The only sure way of success was to loiter in the corridors until he was seen to leave and then grab the girl from where ever you had hidden her and rush to your room.

Frank was not content with a one night stand and managed to conceal one of the village girls in his room for several days. It would have been longer but she was sprung by the Chief when taking a bath in the men's bathroom. Even then she was not discovered living in the male quarters just a "cousin" visiting who had fallen on the dusty drive and had been offered the opportunity to freshen up.

Outside of the male resident staff quarters was the hospital clock tower. A masterpiece of Victorian architecture and engineering it was a local landmark and easily seen from the village. Unfortunately the villagers didn't have to live in close proximity to it as we did.

The clocks great drawback was that it chimed every hour between 6-00 am and midnight. As the hour approached the clock's gears could be heard clanking away until the clapper hit the bell and the time was struck off. It would take all of a minute for this cumbersome system to chime seven-o-clock. At first I found it a great source of irritation but after some sleepless nights I learned to shut out the din and ignore it.

The clock tower was the only thing in the resident staff quarters that Frank hadn't assimilated into his system. Every thing else worked for him. For a small sum of money a trusted worker patient cleaned his room, ironed his clothes and did personal shopping. Another patient collected his shoes in the evening and returned them clean and ready to wear the following day. In order to avoid the loathsome bathroom rush, Frank would leave his ablutions until after breakfast and while some of us utilised our precious 3/4 hour break from the ward to tidy our rooms ready for inspection, he would take a bath knowing his 'worker' would keep the room tidy.

Like many students, working long hours and then drinking at the pub or staff club late into the night, Franks' biggest problem was getting out of bed in the mornings. Most of us had the same difficulty but for Frank, lying in bed was almost an obsession. He loathed dragging himself in the early morning from his warm pit and out into the cold, often dark, corridors which led to the wards.

Sunday evenings, living in, had it's own ritual. We'd all dash off the wards and crowd into the common room to watch "*Sunday Night at the London Palladium.*" The show usually featured some big named star or pop group which most of us wanted to see. There was much good natured banter as we all arrived in a rush to try and secure the prime seats in front of the telly. Before the main act came on the compare of the show, held a 'give away game' with a catch phrase of *"You have sixty seconds to beat the clock. Starting from now."*

Most of us talked throughout this part of the show, arranging what we would do when the programme was over, but not Frank. He seemed to derive a perverse satisfaction from the banalities of the game and would sit on the edge of his seat, eyes glued to the television.

I was off duty and lying in my bed waiting for the clock to chime and tell me what time it was. My alarm clock had stopped and I wanted to get up for breakfast. It would have been a simple matter to have gotten up and looked at my watch on the dressing table but my bed was warm and snug and it was cold outside.

I knew it was after six because the noise of the early morning clamour for the wash room had wakened me. Now the block was silent as most people headed for the wards. I was in that state of dozing and waking where there's no sense of time, just a warm and comfortable bed.

The gears of the clock began to rattle and groan their way to the first chime-'bong'. 'Crash' I was jolted to wakefulness by an unholy racket coming from the room next door. I heard Frank yell.

"You have sixty seconds to beat the clock starting from now."

There was the sounds of frantic opening and slamming of drawers and cupboards interspersed with curses and the steady bong of the clock. The slam of a room door and the heavy pounding of feet racing along the corridor.

I was wide awake, out of bed and up to the room window in time to see Frank running along the main hospital corridor. He reached the ward door and had his keys in the lock just as the clock chimed the last stroke of seven.

At last Frank had found a system for getting up in the morning. He even had the bloody hospital clock working for him. Beating the clock became part of Franks' daily routine when he was on duty. It only failed him once. One morning, in his haste, he mistook his black pajama trousers for his uniform and only when he reached the ward door and went to put his keys in his trouser pocket did he realise his mistake. That day—he was late.

The second year of training in the hospital is always one of the most enjoyable for the student. Not so new that everything is strange, the pressure of the first year examinations is over and the finals seem a long way off. It is a year for practical jokes, girls and boisterous behaviour. A time for cementing friendships and living hard. Dave Sugden, one of the students in our group, Frank, my next door neighbour, and I had developed a close friendship. This was helped along because fate had placed us on the same roster and consequently our days off duty all fell together.

Dave was fat, Frank was tall and athletic and I was thin and weedy. We hung around so much together the others in the staff block referred to us as the three musketeers or the three stooges. We liked the idea of being musketeers and adopted a suitable all for one—or all for us—attitude. We usually managed to get out of the hospital twice a week to go down to the village pub together. When finances or time conspired against us we'd get to the last hour at the staff social club and nurse a solitary beer.

The larger groups that used to go out on motorbikes during the earlier part of our training had waned. Some had left, others were going steady with girls, and holidays and irregular hours all served to split us up. Now we only went out in large groups during block lectures when we all worked the same hours.

Such was the friendship established between the three of us that we took to looking out for one another at meal times and deciding where to go after work. The choices were made simple. Unless we wanted a long journey into one of the towns, which after a thirteen hour shift could be a pain, our choice was limited to one of the four pubs in the village or the staff club. The village won the vote most frequently if only to rid ourselves of uniforms and the smell of the wards from our nostrils. The village pubs were a one and a half mile walk. There was a bus but it was infrequent and impractical. We used the motorbikes occasionally, but most often we walked, because the walk back to Halley served to sober us up a little. Especially on pay days when there was a tendency to switch from our usual beer to much stronger spirits.

The first of a silly season of jokes started one night on our return from the village when Frank suggested we cut across the fields and enter the hospital through the back gate. It would save risking waking Bert from his kip and having to explain why we hadn't handed our keys in to the gatehouse on the way out. As we crossed the field, less than sober, or as my father would have put it—quite pissed. we found ourselves amongst a herd of cows.

"Rustlers." cried Frank and with a whoop headed off at full tilt in their direction. Dave and I, back to childhood days, slapped our imaginary horses into action, and followed. The cows scattered in every direction, their gentle evening perambulations spurred into action by our noisy revelry. After much stumbling and breathless running we finally cornered a cow against a far wall of the field. We slowed to a walk, three in line, and approached together. The beast seemed to grow in size as the alcohol and inky blackness of the night altered our perceptions.

"Are you sure its a cow." I asked, as we got closer.

"'Course." Frank replied, his breath coming in boozy gasps.

"Look underneath." Was Dave's contribution.

Slowly the three of us bent low and peered at the cows nether regions. In the dark, with the cow up against the wall, all we could see was a dark mass without any form. The cow, less frightened now that the pace had slackened, moved hesitantly towards us. That was enough. The thought of bull firmly planted in our minds. As one we turned and ran, fleeing as though the devil himself was after us, we didn't stop or look back until we'd passed through the gate into the next field.

Down in the pub the next evening we talked over the incident of the bull/cow. We referred to it as a bull because we were reluctant to admit we might have been scared by a cow.

"The trouble was, what could we have done with it even if we'd caught it?" Dave was speaking his thoughts aloud as he pulled on his fourth pint.

"Yes!," Said Frank "We should have gone for something smaller."

"Like a sheep?" I said.

We were warming to the idea again having regained some of the last nights lost courage with a few beers. Anyway the seed was sown.

On the way home later we gave the field with the "bull" in a wide berth and climbed over a wall further on, into a field of sheep. Sheep are a lot faster than cows but we eventually, after much loud whispering, arrived flushed with breathless excitement with one cornered by a gate. Frank removed his tie and quickly looped it over the sheep's head. It was in real terms quite a mature lamb and offered very little resistance.

Triumphant we returned to the hospital with our trophy. It was easier than we'd anticipated getting the lamb across the grounds and up to the second floor of the staff block without being seen. It seemed quite happy in our company and offered no real trouble even climbing the stairs. We turned our charge loose on the second floor and went back down stairs to our rooms on the first. The lamb must have been very quiet, at least while I fell into bed, exhausted from our exertions.

The next morning, as the six-o-clock risers made their usual rush for the bathroom it was a different story. The last thing one expects to see in the bathroom is a lamb, especially first thing in the morning. Likewise it must have been very disturbing for a young lamb to find itself amongst a bleary-eyed group of people with lather all over their faces. The result was a spectacular racket with shouts, yells and the strident bleating of the lamb as attempts were made to catch it. I was off duty and happily lay in bed listening to the din on the floor above.

Frank and Dave, came to my room at breakfast time. They were both working overtime and had gone up stairs to help/hinder the activities of earlier. They'd reasoned that to ignore the noise when they were on duty would have been incriminating. To appear as surprised as everyone else would eliminate suspicions. By lunch time the episode of the lamb was the talking point of the hospital with the rumour it had strayed up stairs during the night being the most acceptable. After a hectic chase the lamb was caught and taken to the children's ward until the farmer came to collect it. It brought delight to the children but not much to the staff who had to clean up the droppings.

No Room for a Lamb

A week later we were occupying our usual table at "The Dog," one of the village pubs, discussing yet again the incident of the sheep in a conspiratorial whisper. We were getting bored. Second year blues someone called it. The finals were a long way off—numbers of students had dwindled and shortage of cash meant visits to the bright lights of Manchester or London were just pipe dreams.

To add to our depression there was a flu epidemic in progress at the hospital which had hit both staff and patients. Many of the staff were off sick and we were doubling up on shifts. We'd all worked six thirteen hour shifts of duty without a day off and were tired and losing interest in the job.

"Well, what next?" It was Dave who voiced our feelings.

The episode with the lamb had been such a success that we didn't want to end with just one joke. We needed something outside the wards to break the monotony. Silence prevailed at our table as we went through the motions of drinking our nightly quota of beer. Not one idea between us—it was all too bloody depressing. The next morning I met Dave on the corridors on the way to the wards. He was back to his usual cheery self.

"I've had and idea." He said.

"What?"

"Tell you tonight down the pub. You and Frank go on ahead, I'll meet you down there." Without any further explanation Dave hurried about his work.

Frank and I had finished two pints by the time Dave arrived at the pub all breathless and flushed.

"It took me longer than I thought to find the things we needed." He offered by way of apology.

"Listen." Dave took a long swig at the fresh frothy pint Frank handed him and leaned forward over the table. Frank and I inclined our heads towards him and he put his arms round our shoulders pulling us together into an American Football team huddle. He explained his idea to us in a whisper.

"Fantastic!" was Franks exclamation.

"Great" I added.

The next hour was spent trying to curb our impatience, we wanted to get on with Dave's idea but realised we had to get back to the hospital late. To pass the time away Frank suggested he and Dave win us a few pints of beer at darts. I was to take the chalk and score and they'd ensure that the losers would buy me a drink as well. Frank had spent a lot of time, and money, studying the habits of pub dart players and at one time played in a darts league. Dave had played a lot in the army and together they made a formidable combination. They were hustlers of the highest order.

The secret of much of their success was to lure the opposition into a false sense of security. This was usually accomplished by throwing darts left handed into the board and trying to play a game. Their scores would be appalling and it wouldn't be long before some visitors to the village would offer to play them for a pint. So confident were Dave and Frank of their abilities they'd often deliberately miss the bulls eye and give their opponents the chance to start the game.

They played 301-up with a double to start the game and a double to finish. Once the game was joined they switched to throwing with their right hands and the visitors would be two games down before they twigged what had happened. I once saw them finish a game with only eight darts. Frank started with double twenty and two in the sixty. Dave scored a hundred and Frank ended with a nineteen, double eleven. This occurred before the other team scored their opening double. They weren't always so lucky and some of the games were lost. This didn't worry me unduly, not only did I have confidence in their abilities but I didn't have to pay anything anyway—I was only the scorer.

On this occasion Frank and Dave were good enough to win us all a couple of pints and the waiting time to set our new plan into action didn't seem quite such a drag. The pub closed at eleven and we received our marching orders from the landlord. We bought a few bottles to take back to the hospital and took our time walking back because we knew we couldn't put Dave's plan into action until at least after midnight.

Once back we sat in Dave's room drinking the bottles, playing records and talking. We didn't sit in the lounge because we didn't want anyone to associate the three of us with being up late. About half past twelve the whole staff block was silent save for the muted sound of a radio playing in someone's room along the corridor.

"About time," said Dave, sotto voice. And quietly sprang up from the bed. Lying on the floor and reaching underneath he dragged out about a hundred and fifty yards of coiled nylon rope.

"Give us a hand, it's heavy." He grunted.

The three of us struggled with the weight of the rope. It was quite thin stuff but in this kind of quantity it seemed to weigh a ton.

"Where did you get it?" I asked.

"Under the stage in the hall."

It was one of the ropes used for lifting the props on the stage.

"I had a hell of a job getting it up here without anyone seeing me. I had to pinch a wheelchair from the children's ward to transport it"

Dave was now trying to coil the rope into some form of order

Leaving Dave's record player to quietly work its way through Elvis' Golden Hits, the three of us hauled the rope up the stairs to the floor above. With shoes off, quietly and stealthily we roped all the door handles of the staff rooms on the second floor together. Elvis was just disappearing down the hole in the middle of the record as we finished the job and returned to Dave's room. One last beer and then tip toe to bed.

All three of us were on duty the next morning and together with most of the student staff from the first floor went up stairs to investigate the commotion. Curses and swearing greeted us as the usual frantic rush was replaced by a rising frustration. Guys were getting their doors half open only to have them slammed shut as their neighbours also tried to leave their rooms. The whole event only lasted about five minutes until a desperate tug by one of the 'inmates' pulled off his door handle and gave others enough slack to free their own doors and get out. The staff on the second floor knew the joke was done by *someone from down below* and dire reprisals were threatened against us all. We waited in anticipation for days but nothing happened.

A few weeks after the incident of roping the doors together we arrived back from the pub early. It was nearing pay day and cash was getting short. Collecting three coffees from the kitchen we took them up stairs to the staff lounge to drink at leisure. No one was in the lounge, which wasn't unusual for a mid week night. We flopped into three armchairs to sip our coffee and talk about the wards. Frank was sitting in a chair near the window and as we talked looked out over the hospital drive from time to time.

Suddenly he stiffened then jumped up.

"Follow me—quick."

Dave and I raced after him as he pelted for the second floor landing. By the time we'd caught up with him he'd reached the open window by the stairwell and was peering out into the blackness. We craned our necks to see round him and find out what was attracting his interest. I could just make out a figure in male nurses uniform walking along the drive.

"It's only old Bill Smethers." I said.

Bill was a ward assistant with some 25 years of service and could regularly be seen, twice a week, wending his inebriated way back to the staff quarters after a night out. Assistants were paid less than trained staff but Bill had a few bob put by from his army pension and always seemed to have enough to indulge in his simple pleasures of horses, women and booze.

Frank was tugging at the fire hose reel on the wall,

"Let's ambush him.," he whispered.

Dave parted the curtains smoothly and silently as I turned the wall valve and Frank opened up the hose on the figure below.

"What the fucking hell!" there was a pause like eternity as the sound of the voice sank in and realisation dawned on us.

"Bloody Nora!—It's the Night Super."

Frank dropped the hose in fright and all three of us legged it down the stairs to our bedrooms as fast as we could go. I didn't even pause to undress, just jumped into bed and pulled the covers over me. I hoped it would look like I was sleeping.

After about a million years passed without a sound I gingerly climbed out of bed and undressed. Now the surge of adrenaline had subsided I flaked out like a light. It felt as though I'd only just gone to sleep when a pounding on the door woke me up. A glance at the clock said it was half past three. I must have slept for at least two hours.

"Cummon, wake up." It was the night superintendents voice.

Sleepily I opened the door and was at once blinded by the corridor lights. Blinking through watery eyes I slowly became aware of the gathering behind the super. He had wakened nearly every student in the staff block and they were all standing behind him cold and sleepy in their pajamas. I caught sight of Dave making himself as inconspicuous as possible at the back of the group. There was no sign of Frank. Being a post graduate the super had not thought to wake him.

"This way." Growled the night superintendent as much to the rest of the group as to me.

He set off down the stairs. As we reached the end of the corridor I realised what had happened. I'd thought that the Super was being a bit extreme about his soaking—but now I saw it. In our haste to get away we'd forgotten to turn off the fire hose. A waterfall had been running for several hours down two flights of stairs and into the Chiefs Office at the bottom. After his soaking the night Super had continued on his rounds, stopped off at his house on the staff estate for a change of clothes and drink a mug of cocoa, before returning to his office.

The hose had been running for at least two hours. On his return the Super had found the flood and promptly set about waking up the students.

"Right,. he turned to face us. "I don't know which one of you bloody students it was, but you can all clean it up."

Dave and I acted as dumb as the rest over what had happened and grumbled along with them about having to clean up the mess. It is no joke working in a cold hospital corridor with a mop and bucket, at three thirty in the morning, wearing only your pajamas. If we'd confessed any knowledge of the incident we would have been in serious trouble with all the students on the block.

Frank was highly amused about the whole affair the next morning at breakfast.

As Dave said.

"He didn't bloomin well have to clean it up."

The spree of practical jokes came to an abrupt end several weeks later. That is to say, our involvement with them. Other groups were in action with a similar sense of humour and when I look back at life on the residential block it seems there was always something going on. I'd just finished work and was getting ready to go off duty in the ward locker room when Frank and Dave walked in. They'd both managed to get off a few minutes early and were hoping we could go out as usual.

"Sorry," I said, "not tonight. I've someone to visit on the staff estate."

In fact I had a heavy date with a nurse that I'd been trying to get to know for several weeks but it wasn't a wise thing to broadcast such information. In our group of boozing friends, birds came second to alcohol except on Saturday nights.

Aw!, Cummon." Dave persuaded. "If you're short of cash I can lend you some."

I felt awful. It was a great sin to miss going out with the lads and for a girl. I was nearly at the point of changing my mind when I remembered the only other time I'd got this nurse to go out with me. I had come very close to chatting her into bed and had great expectations this time of getting my end away. My father's advice was still ringing in my ears.

"Don't bring any trouble home with you. It'll upset your mother."

I had no wish to upset my mother so this one and only aspect of parental sex-education continued to prove very useful. Hadn't I visited the barber earlier this week to obtain another packet. I certainly didn't want to waste them.

Suddenly I felt very horny and drinking with the lads paled into insignificance.

"No. Sorry fella's—I promised." I was now full of resolve.

The lads looked a bit down. We'd always gone out as a threesome. I felt guilty like the ground should open up and swallow me for not being open and honest with them. In the end I offered a compromise.

"Look, if you're back early enough then bring some bottles back and have a drink in the lounge. I shouldn't be late and we can drink just as easily there."

I could feel myself colour up as the lie tripped easily from my lips. There was no way I was going to join anyone in the lounge if my plans for the evening worked out. I was hoping for better things. However, the lie worked. Dave and Frank brightened up a little as their trip to the village would now have a dual purpose. They could have a few drinks and bring some home for me.

"O.K." said Dave, "seeya later."

With that the two of them left the locker room to get changed.

I enjoyed a most satisfactory evening. I walked with the nurse along the river bank at the back of the hospital. She was a couple of years older than me and made all the running after I had plucked up the courage to kiss her. She was one of what we laughingly called the *"redcoats."* They were a group of University Student nurses/Health Vistors from Manchester who came to live and work at Halley for six weeks as part of their course. They were made distinctive because of the red capes which they wore as part of their uniform.

Most of the time they kept apart from the hospital staff and sat, when they were off duty, in a compact group in the staff club. I'd worked hard to separate Andrea (that was her name) from her group shortly after they'd arrived at the hospital. I had used the pretext of showing her the tennis courts one night after drinks in the staff club to get her on her own. They were working to a strict schedule and this was only the second time we'd managed to get together. Apparently, the bonding between her group was as close as that between Dave, Frank and me.

Our first outing together had been when all the others were working and we'd elected to walk to the village and bring back fish and chips. It had been a very close encounter for two people living away from home and family but the inevitable presence of the others on our return interrupted our relationship going any further.

Soon the redcoats would be returning to Manchester and Andrea would be out of reach. So this was my last chance and I was determined to make the most of it. The other girls in her group had decided to go into town to see a film and Andrea had stayed behind on the pretext of wanting to study and have an early night. As we walked and talked I found she'd the same feelings that I had when trying to separate from the group. We sat under the trees on the river bank and talked. There is something romantic about just sitting together, throwing pebbles into a river and watching the ripples spread out in the moonlight.

After that first kiss. It was as though a flood gate opened and in a wave of passion we had sex (although I tended to think of it as making love) because, at that instant I decided I was in love. We walked along the river bank afterwards and as it was still quite early called back at the female nurses home for coffee.

The female nurses quarters were situated at the back of the grounds well away from the wards and everything else. They were guarded by an Assistant Matron who lived on the ground floor near the front door. Andrea—ever resourceful—borrowed a fire escape key from one of the other students. I was tingling with excitement at this adventure. The female quarters were much nicer than the Spartan male staff block. They even had their own wash hand basins in every room. Andrea went first and when the coast was clear beckoned me down the corridor into her room.

She left me sitting on the bed while she went to the kitchen at the end of the corridor to make coffee. I sat on the bed feeling awkward, examining the room with wide eyes. Women's rooms are so much nicer than men's. There was a softness about everything, even the furnishings.

My adrenaline was up, causing my senses to be heightened Every time there was a movement in the corridor outside I prepared to bolt for it.

After what seemed like a lifetime Andrea reappeared with the coffee. Her presence had a calming effect and we lay on the bed in the darkness talking in whispers and sipping our coffee. It was infinitely preferable to river banks or the orgasmic fiascoes of the bus shelter on a Saturday night. I was not exactly a virgin but my other sexual encounters in bedrooms occurred with one eye out for interruptions from parents, brothers, sisters and more recently hospital friends. Here with self confident Andrea, in the security of her room, I was able to relax and enjoy but I still remembered to follow my father's advice.

About eleven o clock I walked back to the male staff quarters. I begged the loan of the fire escape key from Andrea to have my own cut. One never knew when such a thing might come in handy. I was walking up in the clouds. An accomplished lover, a man of the world. I'd completely forgotten about Frank, Dave and the beer.

I was in bed sound asleep when a gentle tap, tap, tapping permeated through my sex exhausted sleep and roused me to consciousness. I held my alarm clock up and squinted at the luminous dial. Two in the morning—Hell—there it was again—it was my room door.

"What." I called sleepily in a hushed voice.

"Drinkie time." Came the muffled, giggly reply. I heard the chink of bottles being gently tapped together. When I'm dead asleep and woken suddenly the last thing I need is a drinkie. Especially when those offering it are obviously miles ahead of me in the consumption stakes. Frank and Dave had stayed on at the pub until closing time and had gotten caught up in an after hours drinking and dominoes group. The landlord of "*The Dog*" could occasionally be persuaded to open up the back room for the locals after the visitors had all gone.

There had followed some heavy drinking and yarning until the early hours. Frank and Dave hadn't left the pub until one in the morning. With dogged loyalty they hadn't forgotten their absent friend and had brought some bottles back. When you're as drunk as a skunk and feel good then it follows that the whole world must feel the same way you do. Through their beery haze Dave and Frank were trying to be considerate to the other staff by talking and giggling in whispers. At the same time trying to honour their debt to me by bringing home the beer. The fact that I would be asleep and disinterested hadn't entered into their thinking.

"Do you two know what time it is?" I asked in a loud whisper.

"Nope." Came a voice from the other side of the door.

"Two-o-clock."

"Gosh." Came the drunken reply, "better have a drink."

"Go away, I'm tired."

"Nope." The bottles clinked—then whispers too faint for me to hear—footsteps retreating down the corridor.

I'll explain to them in the morning I thought and settled back to sleep. Before I could get back to my dreams however there was more noise outside the door. The boys were back.

Ah well. I thought, I'd better get up and have a drink with them before they wake the whole block. I started to wearily clamber out of my pit and reach for the key in the lock. At the precise moment I reached out flames shot through the keyhole. I dropped the key like a hot potato. Still half asleep I was unsure of what was happening. More flames arrived this time under the door. The smell of lighter fluid filled the air as I grabbed a towel from off the back of a chair and beat at the flames. Flicking on the lights I picked up the key from the floor and opened the door.

The paint work on the outside was smoldering. Frank and Dave were on their hands and knees outside the door. Frank was squirting petrol from a *"Ronson"* tin over the door and Dave was igniting it with his lighter.

"You bastards." I hissed, still beating at the now receding flames. Two pairs of doleful drunken eyes looked up at me.

"Good, you're up, come and have a drink."

Although I was angry I must admit I admired their persistence. The thought of the beer outweighed any consideration for the door, and as I was up I might as well have one. Pausing to make sure the fire was out we adjourned to the lounge. Six bottles later I went off to bed leaving Frank and Dave sprawled over a couple of chairs where they'd fallen asleep.

It wasn't until I got up for work later that morning that the full extent of the damage was apparent. The lino under the door was only slightly bubbled and charred but, horror of horrors, both sides of the door were a mess. Varnish had blistered and lifted and the wood was charred black underneath. It looked beyond repair. I dashed along the corridor and woke up Dave and Frank. They were both day off and reluctant to get out of bed but my obvious concern finally got through to them.

"Look at my door. What if the Chief does a round of the staff block? How can I explain it?" My voice was rising to an excited squeak as I spoke.

Frank and Dave stood silently surveying the damage caused by their drunken revelry of the early morning.

"We're off duty today mate, leave it with us," Frank gave me his not to worry smile. I looked at my watch. It was time to go on to the wards.

"Don't forget." I was pleading with them.

"No sweat." said Dave.

Feeling no better I went off to the ward. It would be at least an hour before I would be able to come back for breakfast and check on how they were going. The early morning duty dragged and I found it hard to concentrate on getting the patients dressed. All I could think of was the damaged door and the possible repercussions if the Chief found out. I thanked the God who looked after students and who had abandoned the Chief's room inspections some time ago when it was getting harder to attract new staff into the service.

Frank and Dave were waiting for me in the dining room when the charge finally let me off the ward for breakfast.

"Fixed it." said Dave as I sat down to join them.

"Already?" I asked

"No, not yet, but we're going to the paint store to borrow some sand paper and varnish as soon as we've eaten."

Dave looked pleased they'd found a solution to the problem. I couldn't bring myself to go to my room after breakfast in case I met someone on the corridor and they asked me about the fire. Instead I had an extra cup of coffee and cigarette in the dining room and went back to the ward. All morning I was on edge. Every time the telephone rang I paused in what I was doing. It was bound to be the Chief wanting to see me. I worked with one eye on the clock wishing the lunch break would come round soon so I could check on the progress of Frank and Dave. I was ashamed of myself for not trusting them but at the same time knew them for a reckless pair of bastards who didn't really give a toss for authority and could easily stuff up any job. At the back of my mind was the knowledge they would be finding it hard to concentrate on anything. It was their only day off and the pubs would be opening at eleven o clock.

I was dashing along the corridor having been told to go and get my lunch by the charge when I ran slap into Alf doing a round.

"Well Gordon Lad," he said. "I don't exactly approve—especially since you didn't ask permission. Still, I suppose it makes a change having someone interested in their room. I wouldn't have chosen it myself, but your the one who's got to live with it. You must check in future."

Alf had barely come to a halt all the time he was talking. Now he was picking up speed again and heading off towards the wards. I continued in the opposite direction. In less of a hurry now. I had the feeling the Chief's had seen the door after it's repair and that they half approved. But, what did Alf mean—*"I've got to live with it?."*

I bumped into Dave and Frank by the dining room door. They were on their way to the staff club. Having missed their pre-lunch drink they were going for the afternoon session.

"We did it—and the Chief knows." they said in chorus.

"Yes—I've seen Alf" I replied.

"It was the best we could do." said Dave. "The paint shop was low on varnish—but we sanded off the bubbles."

"It looks OK." added Frank.

I wanted to go up to my room before lunch but somehow that would be like breaking faith with the lads. There would be time enough after my meal. Dave and Frank went off to the club and I sat alone at our usual table in the dining room. Was I imagining it or were one or two of the staff talking in whispers and looking in my direction. I began to feel acutely self-conscious. Leaving the rest of my lunch uneaten—I hurried upstairs to my room. It was just as Dave had said. They'd managed to sand all the bubbles of burnt paint off the door and repainted it. The problem was, as there was no varnish, they had used the only paint available to them.—Bright Canary yellow.

It was going to be a long time before I would be able to live this one down. As I said the practical jokes seemed to end as far as we were concerned after that. I'd some how lost my taste for them.

Chapter 10

The Chain Gang

The other ward transfer during my second year was to ward 8. The ambulant epileptics ward. In addition to epilepsy the patients, for the most part had a severe intellectual disability. The usual staff shortages persisted on this ward. Four staff each day were expected to care for eighty patients.

This was only my second occasion at trying to care for adult intellectually disabled patients and the severity of their handicaps came as something of a shock to my system. Sixty of the men slept in one huge room. The beds were only six inches off the floor to lessen the impact if one should have a seizure and fall out of bed.

When I opened the ward door, the overpowering smell of incontinence, sweat and stale breath polluted by medication, could be cut with a knife. The first thing the staff did, no matter how cold the weather, was to open all the windows.

The day I arrived on the ward it was shaving morning. The patients were only shaved on alternate days and growing a beard in the institution was not allowed.

As usual with a ward change I reported to the charge at seven in the morning. The cold rain and darkness outside on the open corridor made the stale odour of a ward where eighty people had slept in one dormitory just about bearable.

The charge took me into the staff room and found me a locker. The other two ward staff were already changed into the inevitable white jackets and as I walked in poured a welcome cup of tea. My locker had three serviceable jackets in it so I selected one and put it on.

"What's on this morning?" I asked.

"Shaving." Replied the monosyllabic deputy charge who was sitting in the only arm chair grasping his mug of tea to warm his hands.

"I'm going on first breakfast and I expect you two to have finished by the time I get back." He nodded towards a jovial looking nursing assistant sprawled, legs outstretched on a cane backed chair leaning against the wall. The deputy strode out of the locker room, white coat unbuttoned billowing behind him as he went to discuss the day with the charge nurse.

The nursing assistant winked at me and his face erupted into a broad grin. He stood up and moved towards me proffering his hand.

"Arnold Briggs," he said gripping my hand firmly." Everyone calls me Art. Welcome to the land of the lost."

Art was a most likable man. He'd joined the hospital staff direct from the army and having no inclinations to academics declined the opportunity to become a student nurse and settled for the nursing assistant's role. His years in the Grenadier guards had taught him how to keep a low profile, managing to avoid the worst of the jobs and yet achieve the reputation of being a useful worker by making sure what he did do was noticed by those in authority. He'd become something of a permanent fixture on ward eight, and as successive roster and ward changes were posted on the notice board his name continued to crop up in the same place.

Art was to become a good friend in the weeks that followed easing me into the ward routine and helping me over that awkward transitional phase when I felt I didn't belong.

"Well, young fellow" he said, "time to start."

"How many patients need shaving?" I asked.

"Oh, about ten can manage themselves." Art replied airily over his shoulder as he walked out of the room with me following in his wake.

I was mentally wrestling with a problem. Ten could shave themselves, that left seventy people needing shaving—thirty five each. Even if we only took five minutes a patient it would take seventy five minutes. I looked at my watch. Seven fifteen. The deputy would return from his breakfast at eight fifteen. We'd never do it.

Art knocked and walked into the charges office with me still following.

"Shaving gear Mister?" It was both a question and a statement.

The charge nurse just nodded and carried on with what he was doing at the desk. It looked like picking horses out of the racing paper to me. Art opened the cupboard and took out a tray. It contained two shaving mugs with soap, two brushes that had seen better days, and two safety razors. He passed the tray over to me and went over to the charge nurse.

"Blades?"

I was beginning to realise this was an alternate morning ritual. The charge nurse fumbled with his keys below the desk. Studiously he selected one and opened the desk drawer. He pulled out a new packet of ten razor blades and opened it. Slowly he counted out five blades and placed them in Arts outstretched palm.

I followed Art out of the office and walked with him along the corridor towards the ward wash rooms. As we walked Art fished inside his white coat to his waistcoat pocket beneath. He withdrew his hand clutching a used razor blade of the same make as those the charge gave him and swapped it with one of the new ones.

"One for me." He said.

That left us with four new razor blades to shave seventy patients. Art carefully handed me two unused blades and said, as if to reassure me.

"Keep turning them over."

As we neared the washrooms Art yelled at the top of his voice.

"Shaving."

I was to learn later the functions of this ward were carried out with simple economy of language. We used only commands and statements.

As if by magic five worker patients appeared. One was carrying what looked to be a toilet roll. Art noticed me looking at it doubtfully.

"For cuts." He said simply, "as the blade gets older we tend to cut them more."

One of the worker patients took the tray from me, handing back the safety razors. He and another patient took a soap mug and brush each. Five chairs were assembled in the wash room in front of the five wash basins. Each one was just far enough away from the sinks and each other to allow a person to move round it in comfort. I watched Art and copied him as he unwrapped one of the new blades and fitted it into his razor. I noticed as I took the paper off the name 'Wardona' and the legend on the wrapper 'use once and discard.'

"Right" said Art, nodding to one of the workers.

The worker patient disappeared out of the room and reappeared in a flash with ten patients. They stood like mute puppies in the pet shop window. Imploring with their eyes. The shaving ritual was part of their lifestyle and they knew what was expected of them. It was a sort of passive role. Their duty as patients was to be done to. There was an unwritten rule at Halley hospital

"THE COMFORT OF THE STAFF IS THE PATIENTS FIRST CONSIDERATION."

Five of the patients were sat down in the chairs and five stood against the wall to wait their turn. There was no formal introduction of me to my new charges. Not even to the worker patients. I was wearing a white coat, therefore I was a nurse. Anything else it seemed was unnecessary.

The seventy nine severely intellectually disabled patients, although ambulant, had no say in the way in which their life was conducted. The plight of this group shocked me more than any other group in the institution. They seemed to be the great unwanted section of society. Dressed in clothing that was ill fitting and rarely ironed, the reason given was that it facilitated easier removal from the incontinent and fewer laundry problems. Many of the residents wore what appeared to be old black motor cycle crash helmet to protect them when they fell in seizure. Most bore scars under the chin and over the eyebrows where sudden contact with the floor during a fit had caused lacerations which needed stitches. Seeing this pathetic little group herded into the toilet annex like frightened cattle at an abattoir only hardened my resolve to improve their lot when ever I could.

However, this was not the place, nor had I the power to change the world. Miracle Working was getting further and further away. My task for the moment was shaving.

The hot water taps were kept running and the lather brushes flew across faces. Two lather brushes, two shaving mugs, and never a hint of cross infection, barbers rash or any other skin problem.

I positioned myself in front of one of the chairs and a bum with a lathered face was sat in it. I shaved the patient carefully, thinking how easy it was, the blade was new. It was a good shave. I'd been careful to avoid cutting the patient determined not to use the toilet roll. I straightened up feeling proud of myself and glanced across to Art for some reassurance. He had his back to me and I realised I had a lot to learn. His hands moved deftly six bold strokes and he straightened up—patient shaved.

"Next," he called out and another bottom was put in the seat as he moved on to another lathered patient.

I couldn't believe his style. Two strokes of the blade for moustache and cheek. One very bold stroke starting at the left sideburn, descending under the chin and completed at the right. A final flourish of three upward strokes of the blade under the chin and the patient was shaved. He was working at a rate of at least three shaves to my one. I turned back to my patient. He'd gone and another lathered up face had already taken his place.

The patient I'd been working on had been taken away to have the soap washed from his face and toweled dry. I bent back to the task trying to increase my work rate. Face after face flashed before me. Each one with two days beard growth on it and a mountain of creamy lather. I diligently turned the blade over after each shave. After the fifth it became more and more difficult to remove the stubble. I was doubtful the blade was having much effect at all and decided to change blades after twelve patients. So far, at least, I hadn't cut anyone. Twelve came and the new blade lightened my stroke, thirteen, fourteen, fifteen, sixteen. My back was aching from the constant bending, the room was full of steam from the hot running taps and the air was heavy with the smell of shaving soap.

"Last one." Called arts voice out of the mist.

I couldn't believe it. He'd continued to work at his pace of more than three to my one. I looked at my watch. Eight-o-clock. Over Seventy patients in forty five minutes—it didn't seem possible. I was elated as we went off to get our breakfast and then I noticed some of the patients still had little tufts of stubble where the razor blade had missed and almost as many sported little bits of toilet paper. Mostly, I'm glad to say, a product of Art's lightening shaving technique. I pointed out the missed bits to Art as we returned the shaving "kit" to the Charges Office.

"We'll get them next time." was Arts laconic reply. "They don't go anywhere that matters and no one comes to visit anyway."

We went off to breakfast with the Charge Nurse leaving the patients to be watched over by the deputy and a few worker patients. Being responsible for over seventy people with severe epilepsy did not worry him at all. It was rather like a shepherd with a couple of faithful sheep dogs tending his sheep.

During breakfast I learned that Art too didn't approve of all that went on in the wards. His service training had taught him you could change things for the better while appearing to comply with the rules.

One of the ways he managed to shave faster than me was because he always brought in a supply of his own *'Gillette's'*.

The ploy with the exchanging blades on the gallery was to keep up the pretense of working well within the hospital system.

Art and me returned to the ward from breakfast at nine and reported to the charge.

"Keep your coats on." He said, "your taking them all for a walk."

We left the office and walked towards the day room. Art didn't look happy.

"Don't you like walking?" I inquired.

"Not with this lot." Art replied.

The thought occurred to me that with only ten patients who were in any way capable of self motivation the taking of all eighty on a walk was going to be a formidable task. Other minds had already evolved a system. The deputy charge was coming for a walk with us and he already had his overcoat on as we arrived in the day room.

"Boots on—chain gang." The command rang across the room.

Immediately the day room came to life. Worker patients lined up the 'duds' and as fast as Art and I called out their names the workers collected heavy outdoor boots from us and crammed them onto reluctant feet. Very few of the boots has laces it them. Worker patients don't do laces. A similar procedure was used to outfit everyone in a heavy outdoor coat from the racks lining the room. It wasn't quite a "one size fits all" situation but coats would often be a size or two larger than needed or far too short for a tall skinny person.

When everyone was ready the patients were lined up in twos by the ward back door. Extra worker patients arrived. They'd been drafted from the ward up stairs to help take us out. The mass of patients was held back while the door was unlocked and several of the worker patients were sent out with what appeared to be a bundle of sticks and ropes.

The bundle was placed on the floor of the airing court and unrolled to reveal an enormous rope ladder over a hundred feet long. Each rung of sticks and rope formed a slot approximately one yard square. The severely disabled patients were then taken outside two at a time and 'slotted' into the 'rungs'.

When everyone was in place five worker patients in the frontand ten worker patients at the back lifted up the device. Involuntarily those patients caught in the rungs grasped the bar in front of them. Art and I were stationed by the deputy, one on either side of this bizarre column. He was going to bring up the rear.

The popular T.V. programme of the day was a western called 'Rawhide' and the deputy charges face split into a huge grin.

"Head em up—move em out."

The command was yelled in his best Clint Eastwood style.

The worker patients at the front pulled for all they were worth and the group at the back shoved. Eighty pairs of booted bodies were grudgingly pulled or pushed into movement and the vast juggernaught of people got underway. I looked back along my side of the moving column. At the rear we were being followed by five more worker patients pushing wheelchairs. Art caught my glance.

"In case of fits." He called, between the gaps of bobbing heads. "That's why we're on the sides."

Once the chain gang was moving it took up to fifty yards to stop it. That was with the rear group digging their heels in and the front workers backing up into the mass behind. It was obvious that any patient who had an epileptic seizure and fell between the rungs of this exercising machine would be trampled under foot.

The task of the two staff on the side of the column was to be ready to dash in and pull from under the shuffling feet any unlucky victim. Such was the staff shortage that the small army of wheelchairs served to keep staff up with the chain gang rather than have them ferrying those unfortunates who had fits back to the ward. On a bad day the juggernaught would return with several of its rungs empty and patients stacked up two to a wheelchair.

As we got into our stride the moans of protest from the severely disabled patients died. We became a steadily moving procession, silent save for the sound of over eighty pairs of boots shuffling in unison.

This patient powered machine could be seen most days walking it captive charges up and down the back roads of the hospital. It became part of my daily routine while I worked on ward eight.

The Charge nurse never came for a walk with us. He was far too busy managing an empty ward.

It was a group of students who, several years later, managed to put an end to the chain gang. Protests to the chiefs office had no effect. Especially as we couldn't suggest a way of getting all the patients to exercise with so few staff. Anyway, we were only students. A drastic remedy was called for.

Staff sickness left the chain gang short of trained nurses and the task of being in charge of the device fell to a third year student nurse. Instead of confining his activities with the gang to the back roads of the hospital he directed the whole group to the main drive. Once there he had the shuffling mass continue to the central administration building and then proceeded to march them round the flower beds in front of the physician superintendents windows for the whole afternoon.

I think the sight, coupled with the noise of the boots eventually got through to him. I'm told the conversation over the phone was:

"I've seen it."

I don't believe it."

"Get rid of it."

The chain gang was stopped forthwith—and was never seen again. Although we were all glad to see the demise of the chain gang—for many of the inmates of ward eight it meant that their world has shrunk to a ward, and an airing court for the rest of their lives.

The Chain Gang (Note the wheelchairs)

Chapter 11

The Fire Brigade

Because of its sprawling size, and general isolation from any major city, the hospital ran its own fire brigade. It was reasoned that the local Country Fire brigade was part time and would not be able to manage an institution of over two thousand beds. The earliest response from a city brigade would take a least a thirty minutes by road.

To be a member of this elite group was a much sought after job. Not only for the extra ten pounds a year fee offered tax free by a grateful hospital, but for the amount of time fire brigade members were allowed off the wards to practice their fire drill.

There were two distinct fire brigades operating at the institution during my time there:-

The Mark One

Old Sam was the fire chief when I first started work at the institution. He was in his early seventies if he was a day. A good politician around the hospital he'd always managed to use the grace and favour clause in his contract and get re-appointed every year by the review committee. In the early sixties there was no such thing as compulsory retirement. The institutions had a hard enough time keeping staff as it was. However, staff over the age of 65 years had to apply to a review committee each year in order to keep their appointment.

Sam was a full time fire chief and had no other duties. A single man, he'd joined the health service when he was too old for active duty in the County fire brigade. He counted it a stroke of pure genius to have landed the plumb job at the hospital.

The years had been kind to Sam and he was sprightly for his age. I considered him rather small for a fireman being a little over five foot seven but what he lacked in stature he made up for in style. He walked with a cocky rolling gait giving a hearty smile and hello to everyone he met by pulling the ever present pipe from his mouth and waiving it aloft in a greeting.

By choice, Sam lived in the staff quarters and because of his rank was able to obtain two rooms. One for sleeping and one as a sitting room and study. Having served the hospital for twenty years or perhaps the hospital served him, he was senior enough and specialist enough to enjoy the distinction of having no one but the Medical Superintendent to challenge his actions.

Because of his unique position Sam even went to the length of having his uniforms specially tailored. They were cut in a similar fashion to the Chief Male Nurse and sub-officers but with rows of silver pips and flashes giving him the appearance of a general among the ranks. Sam enjoyed all the comforts of home in his staff room and even went to the extent of using a biscuit tin rigged up with a 150 watt light bulb inside as a bed warmer for cold winter nights.

His days were spent plodding round the hospital checking fire extinguishers, polishing his fire appliance or disappearing into some out of the way tea stop where no one could find him. There was a nasty rumour going round the establishment that his pipe created more smoke than he'd ever seen in a fire.

The hospital fire station was at the end of the male drive. There were even residential quarters for staff to live in when on fire duty *'stand-by.'*

Sam considered this an unnecessary waste of space as all the fire brigade staff lived-in or close enough to return in an emergency. The far sighted hospital management committee had built the fire station strictly in accord with county fire brigade principles by providing the best snooker table in the hospital for the fire quarters.

Unfortunately the committee didn't think it was necessary to provide a decent fire engine. The Mark One fire engine was one of those electric trolleys which the driver walks in front of and controls with a handle.

A sort of glorified milk float.

The purpose of this tender was to carry the ladders, hoses, sand buckets and a small petrol operated pump. The firemen walked behind the engine in twos. If they'd run they would have overtaken the engine.

Despite the obvious lack of support from the management Sam took his duties seriously. The fire brigade practiced regularly and spent many hours cleaning the engine and 'taking it for walks'. All fire alarms were diligently attended usually to find they were false and made by patients braking the alarm glass out of frustration or temper.

Sam developed a set of explicit instructions for fire drills and they were incorporated into the hospital rules.

"When the fire alarm sounds, one member of staff from each ward, other than a member of the fire brigade, will report for instructions to the general store. Members of the fire brigade will report to the fire station."

The alarm was coupled to an old air raid siren inside the clock tower so there was no mistaking when it sounded.

The hospital management committee were making one of their infrequent tours of the grounds and administrative areas. They only visited the wards on Christmas day. The chairman of the management committee asked about fire drills as the group of dignitaries was walking through the general store. Ever loyal to his staff the Physician Superintendent informed him they were good. On which advice the chairman promptly smashed the nearest fire alarm.

The fire was at the general store according to the indicator board in the fire station and most of the staff had turned up at that assembly point well before the fire brigade. A period of some ten minutes elapsed with all the available ward staff present before the firemen arrived. Sam was walking in front of his bright red electric tender, huffing and puffing clouds of smoke from the inevitable pipe as the machine hummed along at a steady four miles and hour. The rest of the brigade were marching stolidly behind. No one knows who started it, but applause seemed to be the order of the day.

The Chairman, having got the fire brigade turned out wanted to see a fire drill in full and suggested the group train their hoses on the roof of the general store some fifty feet away.

It was Sam's big moment. With a great flourish we were all moved away from his fire engine. Rummaging about in the tool box he produced a hydrant key. The highly polished brass ended hoses were quickly connected and two members of the fire crew caught hold of the end of the hose and braced themselves for the massive surge of water which must surely follow.

There was stillness about the crowd now as we waited in breathless anticipation. Suddenly there was a belch from the end of the hose and a gurgling stream of dirty brown water shot out of the end of the pipe all of fifteen feet in the air. It was too much. The crowd of onlookers burst into laughter. Sam went red with embarrassment and started fussing with the engine and the Chairman walked away taking the rest of the management committee with him. Nothing was said to Sam about the farce but his contract was not renewed and he retired gracefully.

Like the Phoenix rising from the ashes the Mark Two fire brigade was born.

The Mark Two

The new fire chief was called Harry—simply Harry—I don't think he had another name—leastways no one used it. He represented change. Within weeks of his arrival the fire station boasted of a purpose built long wheel base Landrover fire engine. It was complete with extending ladder, two Dennison pumps capable of lots of thrust, a built in 500 gallon water tank and hoses. Painted the inevitable bright red it was a hospital fireman's dream. It even had a bell.

Harry moved into the fire station quarters, appointed a deputy and insisted people took the task of fire fighting seriously. This led to some inevitable resignations from the brigade allowing me to wangle myself a place in the team by using my special relationship with the Chiefs Office. Harry obtained proper uniforms for us including fire helmets and oilskins. With hatchets in our belts, we looked like firemen and he drilled us until we felt like firemen. Unfortunately our enthusiasm exceeded our skills.

A hospital painter using a blow lamp to scrape paint off windows managed to set the sash cord alight inside the window casement. The room he was working in soon filled with smoke and fumes and the alarm was quickly raised. The indication on the board showed it to be a female ward. The on-duty brigade leapt on to the engine and charged through the hospital, bell ringing, straight to the scene of the fire. Such was the height of our enthusiasm for the work and our wish to please, that, finding the ward door locked, we chopped it down with our hatchets before the ward sister had time to open it with her key.

Male staff, including the fire chief, were not allowed keys for female wards. Once inside the ward we connected the hose to the engine and with full water pressure belching a streaming high pressure jet we succeeded in blowing the window straight off the wall.

We did however, manage to put out the fire without loss of life or limb. Feeling quite proud of ourselves we cleaned up our gear and returned to the fire station. It was several days later when we were summoned to a special meeting at the station. Harry had received a letter from the hospital secretary:-

"I would like to thank the members of the fire department for the speedy and efficient way in which they dealt with the recent fire in one of the female wards. However, I have to inform you that the cost of repairing the damage caused by the fire was five pounds and the cost of repairing the damage caused by the fire brigade was thirty five pounds. Would you please be less exuberant with your hatchets."

Harry promptly had this missive framed and hung it in pride of place in the fire station.

The only other memorable fire during my stay at the hospital was when one of the outer barns caught fire on the hospital farm. It was eleven o clock on a cold November evening when the alarm went off. Most of the hospital fire brigade were just wending their merry way home from the staff club—fire fighting staff weren't allowed to leave the hospital environs when "on call."

As usual I was with Dave and Frank and hurriedly took my leave of them and made for the fire station. There is nothing like a fire alarm to assist in sobering up a group and a full turn-out of staff was soon mustered. Grabbing our fire fighting gear we leapt on to the back of our Landrover fire engine.

Harry, as usual, electing to drive. He wasn't the best driver in the world. In fact, many would have argued he was the worst. But, he was the fire chief and none of us could stop him driving the engine. In a state of reckless abandon we careered down the hospital drive, lights flashing and the inevitable bell ringing to wake up all the patients and night staff. As we swerved wildly round the hospital gate and on to the main road one of the crew fell off the back of the truck and knocked himself out on the hard roadway. We screeched to a halt and ran back to our stricken comrade.

"He's out cold." One of the brigade called out to Harry.

"Never mind," shouted Harry above the noise of the fire engine.

"Throw him in the back. He lives on the way and we can drop him off."

Gunning the engine and crashing through the gears Harry sent the machine swaying wildly into the staff estate where our stricken colleague lived. Everyone lurched forward as he clapped on the anchors and brought the engine sliding to a halt outside the front gate of one of the staff houses. The fireman's wife answered the door.

What a sight we must have looked in our oil slicks and fire helmets, the engine lights flashing, motor running, and our now semi-conscious mate carried between us.

"What happened?" Asked the housewife with a worried frown on her face.

"He fell off." We chorused in reply.

"Oh dear." She opened the door wide and stood back to let us all troop in.

"Put him on the settee." Bending over her husband to check that her spouses injuries were not more serious she then turned to face us.

"I'll phone the doctor in a minute just to give him the once over." Then in true north country fashion.

"Would you chaps like a cup-o-tay."

Harry thought for a moment before he replied.

"No thanks love—we'd better not—we're on our way to a fire y'see."

"Oh well! Another time perhaps," The housewife smiled resigned to the fact that the chance for a good gossip had gone wasted.

"Thank you all for bringing him home then."

Running back to the fire engine we roared off into the night leaving our bemused housewife to stand scratching her head in the doorway.

The barn was situated at the top of a large sloping field where, during the summer months we'd spent many happy hours damming up a stream to give us a head of water for the pumps. Not, because we had second sight and were anticipating the fire, but because the local pub was within walking distance and a quick pint could be obtained without being caught.

The gate to the field was closed as we turned off the road and Bob Hardie, the deputy fire chief, jumped down from the privileged seat in the front of the engine to open it. It was inky black at that time of night in the high-hedged entrance to the field and unable to see where he was going Bob stumbled into the ditch. From our vantage point at the back of the fire engine we could see thin tongues of flame flickering above the barn roof. This, coupled with Harry's natural impatience, meant we wouldn't wait for Bob to extricate himself from the ditch. Harry just drove on leaving the crash bars on the front of the vehicle to take care of the closed gate and its hinges.

The plan of action was simple. We'd jump off the engine at regular intervals as it drove across the field and down to the stream. Each of us would carry two lengths of hose which we'd connect up and join to those of our mates in front and behind. Harry was to man the pumps and engine at the stream while the rest of us made our way up the hill to the barn and deployed the hose nozzles with maximum effect.

The field was only marginally brighter than the entrance gate in which we'd lost Bob and visibility was further hindered by the wind blowing the smoke from the fire downhill towards us. Valuable minutes were lost with the entire fire brigade wandering round the field, each with two lengths of hose, looking for someone or something to connect up to.

Eventually we got all the hoses assembled and congregated by the blazing building. Two of the farm staff were on hand and had freed the few cattle who'd been sheltered in the barn for the night. They informed us the place was full of hay and was well ablaze inside. A light was flashed in the general direction of Harry in the vain hope he'd see it and start the pumps.

During practice the water had taken a few minutes to find its way up the hill and we'd developed the habit of grabbing a quick smoke. Harry hadn't told us on those earlier occasions he'd only been working the pumps at half power.

We'd just got the cigarettes lit and were stand with one foot on the hose nozzle when the water burst from the ends of the with the full thrust of twin pumps working under maximum pressure behind it. They soaked all of us thoroughly before they danced off across the field with the fire brigade in full pursuit.

Happily, for our self esteem, we'd restored order and were busily fighting the fire by the time the county fire brigade arrive from the town. Being a rural area the county brigade was mostly auxiliary tenders and part time firemen like ourselves. As a consequence they were quite willing for us to stay and give them a hand.

The highlight of the fire was when a turntable ladder arrived on loan from the city fire brigade. It was to be used to spray water on the roof of nearby farm buildings to stop the fire spreading. The hospital fire brigade members were taking it in turns to relieve various members of the county force and I quickly offered to do a stint up the ladder. In the city I would have been given the bums rush, but this was the country and things are a lot different.

I got my chance about an hour after I had offered and climbed gingerly up the dizzy heights of the ladder. Once at the top I was instructed where to direct the hose and settled to the task from my grandstand view. For two hours I played water onto the buildings nearest the fire, adjusting my direction as instructed by the senior fire officer. It was a fascinating experience and I soon lost myself in the myriad patterns formed by the smoke, steam and flames. It was time for my relief. when my problems started.

The hard night frost and dribbling water from the hose had caused my oilskin jacket to become frozen to the rungs and side of the ladder. I was well and truly stuck. I couldn't jerk myself away from the side of the ladder for fear of falling. I had to stay put and yell for help until someone could find the time to climb the ladder and release me. No one said much when I descended but I still felt a considerable embarrassment, in fact my cheeks were probably hotter than the centre of the fire.

As country fires go, it was a costly blaze and destroyed not only the barn but some machinery and that precious commodity, animal feed, by the ton. We stayed at work on the fire all night and were relieved of all ward duties until the fire was extinguished. We had to report to the fire chief each shift until the fire was judged to be out. In the event, the barn burnt for two days and smoldered for almost a week

Of course the fire brigade was not only concerned with putting out fires but also with fire prevention. This included occasional checks of the hospital grounds, fire extinguishers and in particular the farm and market garden sheds where many combustible materials were stored and a quiet beer could be had at the pub just over the field.

One evening a report was made that a light had been seen in one of the large sheds in the hospital market garden. The memory of the barn fire was still in the minds of many of the staff and this incident couldn't be let pass without investigation. The members of the fire brigade were called quietly by telephone and asked to report to the fire station with the minimum of fuss.

Harry was waiting for us and explained he'd also called the local police and we were going to try and nab the fire bug on the spot. Six burly policemen—the local constable and five specials arrived almost at the same time as most of the fire crew. Harry and the constable had a bloody unholy row as to who was going to command the operation.

A compromise was reached and they decided on a joint plan of action. Both police and firemen were to converge quietly on the barn by rolling the fire engine and police car with engines switched off up to the shed door. We'd be deployed to surround the building and when everyone was in position, the shed door would be flung wide open, the whole area illuminated by the vehicle headlights, and we would catch the fire raising vagrant red handed.

Such are the jungle drums which cause communication in hospitals that by the time we were all in position in the market garden our ranks were swollen by equivalent numbers of resident and night duty staff. Just there to watch of course—not to interfere. It is remarkable that everyone was ushered into place with the minimum of fuss and noise.

"Now." Yelled a voice from the dark.

The door was flung wide open and the lights flicked on. There to illuminate the naked figures of a male charge nurse and female charge sister lying in the hay. He was engaged in pouring the contents of a bottle of wine between her breasts and lapping it up as it pooled round her naval. We all stood rooted to the spot as the naked charge rose sheepishly from his lovers side. The sister was trying to cover her embarrassment with her hands—he covered his with the wine bottle. It was the male charge who broke the silence.

"Nay lads, be decent, turn the lights out while us gets dressed."

The lights flicked out and the crowd melted away like theatre patrons dashing out to escape the national anthem. We took the fire engine back to the station—I would never get another chance to ride on it again for real. I was well into my training now and needed all my spare time for study and parties.

Harry was given the sack some time later. It served him right. He left the fire engine outside the pub when he went for a drink. He should have parked it round the back as usual.

On the way to the farm fire.

Chapter 12

The Female Side of the Hospital

NEVER

NOT UNDER ANY CIRCUMSTANCES

Gordon Kerkham, RN, RNMS, RPN, MNP

ARE MALE STAFF ALLOWED

IN OR NEAR THE FEMALE SIDE OF THE HOSPITAL

Gordon Kerkham, RN, RNMS, RPN, MNP

LET ALONE—NEAR FEMALE PATIENTS.

SIGNED—THE MATRON

Chapter 13

Eurhythmics

The Physician Superintendent gave an inspired talk to the student nurses on the therapeutic value of music and movement.

"If music was used in a structured and ordered way the lives of even the most severely intellectually disabled people could be enhanced."

Victor, a student nurse from Spain, and me were all fired up with enthusiasm. We were getting towards the end of our second year in the hospital and knew our way around. If such a programme was to be established in Halley hospital we needed to short circuit the usual line channels and get straight through to the Chief Male Nurse.

Our task was made easier by old 'Bill the Bastard' being on annual leave and the hospital having just appointed a new Chief. Prior to the appointment Bill was highly fancied for the top position himself. He'd been acting Chief Male Nurse for over a year and acquitted himself well in his terms. Unfortunately he didn't fit in with the hospital social scene and had a tendency to be too abrupt with more senior members of the board. They gave him the courtesy of an interview then appointed an 'outsider'.

The new chief had known the Physician Superintendent for some years and had let him know he wasn't happy in his previous post. A few strings were pulled, a few ears whispered into and Halley had a new Chief. To help the new Chief settle in to the hospital Bill had been asked to take his annual leave.

In this instance, I knew exactly the right approach to use. If the Physician Superintendent thought it was a good idea there was no way a new Chief Male Nurse was going to argue with it. It worked especially when we let it drop that the Super had lectured about it. We were even able to sell the idea that the music and movement group should be carried out in the main recreation hall as part of a student project. As Victor and I had brought up the idea in the first place we were given the initial task of getting it established.

We were allowed time off the wards and allocated two free mornings in the hall. A piano was made available and a record player. The hospital neglected to ask us if we could play the piano and omitted to give us any records. Thanks to some sterling foraging by Mr. Davis in the training school we acquired a stack of old 78's and a voluntary pianist.

To most of the charge nurses, eurythmics was another of them new fangled ideas that gets put in the students heads in the school.

"Still, you 'av got to hand it to the buggers they know how to get out of having to work on the ward."

The new Chief Male Nurse was on our side—the side of the Physician Super—and suggested that in order to get the cooperation of the charges we should select the most unmanageable patients off each ward. We did—and achieved instant popularity for the idea.

"Any fool who was prepared to take the duds off the ward for an hour or two can't be all bad."

Many weeks and a lot of our own time was spent in preparing the programme. 'Listen with Mother' became a regular part of my daily radio listening. Eventually, sure we could make no further improvements to the programme, we started.

Eurhythmics, was easier, and more fun, than we dared hope. From a group of lifeless beings, sitting in their incontinence and being moved about like cattle, or staring into space day after day in the same surroundings. We made people.

The patients responded. First simple marches which required a lot of tugging and pulling on our part just to make a circuit of the hall, then running, jumping and skipping (after a fashion). I felt, and must have looked, like a bloody fool standing in the middle of that vast ballroom with twenty other raving idiots.

We lay on the floor and relaxed, we were trees, woodsmen with axes—anything that could be done in time to music. Our patients were pulled, pushed, cajoled, praised and finally we won their willing cooperation. It was incredible we same nurses were so afraid of being called fools by our colleagues we didn't play games with the patients on the children's wards.

The group grew from strength to strength and with it the quality of the patients lives. The influence of the Superintendent introduced female patients—very suitably chaperoned, to join in the activities. The hospital had taken a great leap forward. Things were being done for and with the 'duds'.

For one hour, twice a week. They were being taken out of the wards, away from the day rooms, and living. What we were seeing was the vanguard of many changes which were starting to happen within the hospital. In many ways it was like the whole institution was fighting itself. We looked for progress while walking backwards looking over our shoulders.

Sometimes institutional progress gets thrown into reverse, often when the programmes are attacked by the financial managers, occasionally through lack of foresight and planning and sometimes through what I call 'institutional opportunists'.

It was the latter which ended the moment of glory for the severely handicapped.

Such was the system of 'dead men's boots' while waiting for promotion in the hospital system, that some staff would resort to almost any device to ensure they wouldn't be passed over when a more senior vacancy occurred. Because the Superintendent was an open supporter of the music and movement group it was obviously a possible promotion gambit. So on to the band wagon leapt *"Your friend and mine." Jumping John Hall*.

John was an assistant Chief Male Nurse who'd achieved his promotion by organising groups of patients to perform pantomimes at Christmas. It was called *'putting on a show'*. Charges did it when telling parents their relative would receive their personal attention. Students did it when they opened the doors for more senior staff. John Hall did it better than anyone. He 'put on his show' literally for the patients, parents and most important of all—the hospital management committee.

John was always the star of the show and the patients were the natural decoration for him to display his talents with the most effect. The programmes he produced always gave credit where it was due.

The first page would read:

A Pantomime	By John Hall
Written	By John Hall
Produced	By John Hall
Starring	John Hall
The entire cast is under the personal supervision	
of	John Hall

The mere detail of all the other people in the show and the host of others who assisted was confined to the inside of the programme or the small print on the back page.

John had been a professional comedian round the Blackpool pub and club circuit before a slump in the entertainment industry had caused him to seek refuge inside the hospital gates. He had some comedy talent and with no competition from the patients could shine in a manner that the clubs denied him.

John, easily able to pull rank on the mere students, started to visit the eurythmics group and give us his advice. Eventually he persuaded the Chief to let him take charge of the sessions and give them more credibility. I don't think any of the students would have objected, as this made administrative sense. However, it would have helped if John had known anything about the subject. Unfortunately his knowledge about eurhythmics could be accommodated on the back of a postage stamp.

As students, we were only just becoming familiar with the concept. John was convinced, that as he was trained, he knew all about it and proceeded to show us.

John Hall could not have differentiated between free expression, structured gross motor training and country dancing to save his life. Enthusiasm in the student group deteriorated and we eventually found we had replaced eurythmics with a couple of country dances. The Grand Old Duke of York and the Hokey Cokey.

The original group of severely disabled patients were soon returned to the wards as unsuitable as they could not grasp the concept of country dancing or moved too poorly and without proper coordination. They were once again the great passed over—not worth taking anywhere group—who wouldn't appreciate anything anyway.

More intelligent patients who already enjoyed some degree of leisure activity were brought in. They were able to understand the *Grand Old Duke of York*. At this point, after a useless protest, Victor and I volunteered to return to the wards, to give other students a turn.

We were happy to leave John to carry on with what had now been christened the "Three Ring Circus." By most of the staff who had recognized the programme as a drive for promotion to a senior position. The day we were due to return to the wards, fate dealt us a kindly blow.

The addition of the Hokey Cokey to the repertoire of the group had the beneficial spin-off of teaching the patients left from right. After weeks of practice it had become quite a passable dance.

On this particular morning the Chief Male Nurse walked into the hall accompanied by the Physician Superintendent and members of the management committee. The superintendent had been giving the committee members a brief talk about what we were doing with the most severely disabled and seemed a little put out when he saw such an able group assembled.

John, ever the opportunist, saw them enter the hall out of the corner of his eye and quickly formed the group into a circle to perform his showpiece—the Hokey Cokey. Departing from the usual routine, John went and stood in the middle of the circle, as demonstrator, leader. Certainly the members of the management committee would see he was in charge and know where to give the credit.

All went well for the first couple of choruses and although not quite what the management committee expected they seemed quite impressed. Then, on the third chorus, as the patients moved back from the centre of the circle, an outsize pair of slightly soiled knickers was lying on the floor at John's feet. The music tailed off as the pianist brought his hands to his mouth to hide his smile. The circle, with no music, stopped dead and stared. I swear Johns blush started at his ankles and by the time it reached his face was verging on apoplexy as he tried to avoid looking down.

The trouble with ladies knickers is, no matter what the size, they do draw the eyes. Suddenly, a short and very overweight patient burst from the ring. Dashing up to John she swept up the pants with pudgy fingers and tucked them down the front of her dress.

"They're mine." She bellowed, holding Johns eyes with her own as if defying him to contest their ownership.

The Physician Superintendent and his party—po-faced—walked quietly out of the hall. Poor old John took this as a sign of disapproval and worried about it for days. Victor and I returned to the wards—laughing.

John Hall eventually entered local politics and was duly elected. This only served to confirm my opinion of our local city council. Most of them were clowns.

Chapter 14

The Bath House

Another of the delights I was scheduled to meet during my time on ward 8 was the ritual of the bath house.

On wards of seventy or more patients it wasn't considered practical to use the two bathrooms built into the dormitory on the ward. Instead we had the bath house. This was a large barn-like building situated near the stores. It was a red brick building with no windows and drew all its light from the roof where, set amongst the gray slates, were reinforced frosted glass panels. The only entrance was through a green painted door on the side of the building furthest from the road. By the side of the door was a small eight by four brass plate which spelled out the buildings purpose. It bore the legend, in gothic script, "BATH HOUSE."

The inside of the building was divided into two rooms. The first, and smaller had an alcove containing a lavatory, coat pegs all round the walls with benches underneath and a trestle table, clean and scrubbed, in the middle. It looked like the changing room of any local football club. A doorway, without a door, led into the larger room. Round the walls of its high roofed interior twenty bath tubs jutted out like porcelain teeth in some gigantic whales mouth. There were two shiny brass taps affixed to each tub. The cold one of these worked freely whilst the tap for the hot water could only be worked with a special key.

The sign said—"*Hot water keys will remain in the nurses possession at all times.*" Bathroom allocation for each ward was once or twice a week. I suppose it depended on how dirty the senior nursing officers thought your patients were. As three or four wards a day used the bath house it was strictly controlled, timetabled and administered by the chiefs office.

The bathing morning ritual started a long time before a ward group got into the building, the whole morning was centered round the event. The bath house roster was posted daily on the notice board outside the subs office. Staff read them before they went off duty the night before in anticipation of their labours the following day.

It was a great crime not to have read the board, especially if you reported to your ward when the chiefs had rostered you for some special relieving duty. Our ward eight must have been a dirty one because we were always rostered twice a week.

Of course, the job of taking everyone to the bath house and bathing them was left to the usual three. The deputy, Art and me.

When we arrived on the ward in the morning the charge would be busy in the office with a list of patients who, in his opinion, didn't require a bath. Generally he'd manage to eliminate about ten of the brighter patients and thus gain a reason for himself to stay behind on the ward and look after them. Occasionally he would request we take the non-bathers with us as he couldn't manage them and the ward as well. I could never understand what he had to manage if we took all the patients with us and the ward was empty. Still, ours was not to reason . . . .

After breakfast the deputy would station himself at a table in the gallery and cut thin slivers of soap from a large bar of sunlight green. Occasionally we'd run out of the green and he'd use bars of the red carbolic soap used for scrubbing floors. Years of practice had enabled him to cut the slivers of soap so thin that he couldn't have improved on his performance even if he used a spoke shave.

Art and I would be sent up to the day room to keep an eye on the patients and roll clean underpants, shirt and socks up in a towel. Forty pairs only, for the continent and brighter patients, the duds just needed clean socks. They were wet so often they were always getting clean clothes anyway.

Ten minutes before our allotted time in the bath house we lined the patients up at the ward front door and counted them. The charge came with us as far as the front door and unlocked it. He'd never take our number for granted and insisted on counting all the patients again.

Occasionally he would count in Art or me and then we'd have to march everyone back inside and have a recount. We walked to the bath house in two's, the worker patients bringing up the rear with the clean clothes in laundry bags.

The bath house had no heating save for that generated by the hot water pipes. For the first group of the day to use the building it could be bitterly cold, for the later groups the air would be moist and smell of sweaty socks, but at least warm. I couldn't make up my mind which of the two was preferable.

On very cold winters mornings when the frost had turned the snow crunchy underfoot it wasn't uncommon for nurses to keep their outdoor clothes on with a white coat over the top. Our deputy used to wear his overcoat, cap and scarf

Once in the changing room the workers set-to undressing the less able patients and hanging up their clothes. Washing was discarded in the large linen bags we'd brought with us. Now and again we had to provide an extra clean shirt for one of the incontinent patients who'd wet himself on the way over to the bath house. Art and I were given a key each for the hot water and sent to fill the baths

"No more than three inches of hot water mind. We don't want to be here all day."

The deputy provided us with a dip-stick to make sure we got the water level right. It was painted red up to the three inch mark.

Our deputy positioned himself in the doorway between the changing and bathroom. He carefully placed a towel on the floor in front of himself and two of the workers set a small card table at his side. The top of the table was covered with the thin slivers of soap he'd so carefully cut in the ward. From the top of his pocket he produced a fine toothed comb and a pencil.

"Ready" yelled the deputy above the noise generated by the running baths and the patients.

The first patient was pushed forward by the workers on to the towel. Out of habit he positioned himself with hands outstretched and fingers spread. The deputy took his hands in his and glanced at both sides of them and then checked between the mans fingers. Bending from the waist he inspected the soles of the feet and between the toes. The patient raised his arms above his head and his axially hair received a few strokes with the fine toothed comb. His pubic hair received the same consideration. Using his pencil the deputy lifted up the patients penis, so that it looked like a plucked chicken on a perch, and peered at his testicles. Popping the comb and the pencil back in his top pocket he straightened up with a grunt.

"Right." He made ticks in the boxes on his bathing list

The patient was directed to the first bath. In that short space of time our phlegmatic colleague had checked for scabies, long finger and toe nails, bumps, scratches and bruises, verrucas, lice, crabs and hernia. If the patients nails required cutting he'd call 'nails' and Art or me would make a mental note of the offending individual and between running the bath water attempt to get the nails cut.

Selected worker patients who were allowed to bath in the ward moved efficiently into the bathroom. Taking the soap from the table they would wash the less able individuals. It didn't take long for the whole place to be filled with bodies, washing, drying, crying with soap in their eyes, or sitting in three inches of water having their nails cut.

The ward was only allowed an hour to complete the process of bathing all our patients. Art and I ran round pulling out plugs, rinsing quickly with carbolic lotion and filling up baths. The deputy charge didn't move from his station in the doorway checking each patient thoroughly with his pencil and comb. Exactly on the hour we'd be ready to leave the bath house and return to the ward. All the patients clean, the bathroom moist and tidy behind us—for a few days at least.

Chapter 15

Grace

One morning, after an uneventful sojourn at the bath house. The ward received a rare visit from the Physician Superintendent. He walked into the day room accompanied by the charge nurse just as me and Art were preparing the patients for lunch.

"Do you say Grace before meals?" inquired the Superintendent of the charge.

"Yes Sir." The charge was well aware of the hospital rules and snapped almost to attention in reply.

His response was true. Our charge, being a stickler for the rule book of the institution, always insisted on saying grace. The order was;

"Stand behind your chairs." Usually bellowed by the deputy although Art and I occasionally got the chance.

The seventy odd patients milling round in the dining gallery would stand behind their chairs in absolute silence. Years of institutional living had taught them that meals would only be served after a period of absolute silence, followed by grace.

The charge, not leaving his chair, would open his office door and poking his head out would call.

"For whayouare aboutorecieve maythelor mayoutruly thankful."

To which the patients would dutifully chorus "Amen" and sit down to eat.

On this day the *"Big Chief"* was present and Art and I could tell things were going to be different.

"Stand behind your chairs." Was said.

Nothing happened.—Louder,

"Stand behind your chairs."

Nothing.—Art bellowed

"Stand behind your chairs."

The effect was electric and the mass moved into its lunchtime position of silence standing behind their chairs in the dining room.

The charge had slipped into his long white nursing coat. He was going to assist with lunch.

He moved away from the side of the Physician Superintendent and stood in the centre of the dining room. There he adopted a posture which he adjudged spiritually appropriate. Hands clasped in front of him, eyes lowered, he bowed his head. Not wishing to get on the wrong side of our boss. Art and I stood one either side of him and followed suit.

Absolute silence reigned.

Before the charge could proceed any further with this charade the ward kitchen door opened to reveal Benny and Jimmy. They were two long standing ward worker patients who's job it was to prepare the plates on the servery ready for the meal. Patients assisting with serving meals was against the "rules" and Benny realising that the Superintendent was present blurted out.

"For Christ's sake shut that bloody door."

Seventy nine patients solemnly responded with "Amen." and promptly sat down in eager anticipation of their dinner.

"I see." said the Physician Superintendent and walked poker faced from the dining room with the red faced charge trailing in his wake.

We never said Grace again after that.

Chapter 16

Sick Bay

As I moved into my third and final year of training I was required to spend some time working in the sick bay gaining clinical experience. I said goodbye to Art and the gang on ward 8 and moved with anticipation to sick bay.

The ward had the reputation for a high standard of nursing care and I approached my placement with some enthusiasm. The sick bay was the clinical ward for the whole of the male side of the hospital. It was the only ward equipped with a sterilizer capable of boiling a syringe—a much more desirable alternative to the pan on the kitchen stove. In some ways—the fact that we had a sick bay—helps to describe the nature of the institution.

Most of the patients in the hospital were not sick in the 'ill' sense of the word but were robust and healthy people. The general population could easily be forgiven for not understanding this because the title hospital has different connotations in the health care setting.

Even visitors to Halley could be forgiven, when they saw the uniformed staff and white coats on every ward, for thinking in terms of traditional illness. Grappling with a notion of an illness which has no physiological symptoms puzzles even the most thoughtful of philosophers. The 'Mind' is an abstract noun, and doesn't really exist. It certainly will not be found in an anatomical text book. It is a vain thing to talk of Mental illness when there is no "Mental" organ to measure. Just a series of behaviours which are uncommon in the general population.

How were they to know that most of the staff clung to their uniforms as if it was a banner declaring to the world—*"look at me—in uniform—I'm not one of the mad patients."*

The sick bay functioned like the infirmary of any large institution or school. Those patients who for any reason were unable to live without medical help in the hospital ward community were transferred to the sick bay.

Thus the ward functioned as a mini hospital for the whole male campus, dealing with everything from, routine minor operations in out-patients, to infectious fevers, to stabilization of diabetes or epilepsy. There seemed to be a tacit understanding in the chief's office that this was the ward to show off to visitors. Consequently it was always well staffed.

The charge was a Registered General Nurse as well as a Mental Health Nurse and used all of his skills in both disciplines to the utmost to ensure the highest possible standard of care. Worker patients were only allowed to undertake domestic duties far removed from patient care. None of the worker patients assisted with shaving or changing in this ward. Student nurses were in the majority and as a general rule enthusiasm reigned. It was here we were allowed to practice some of the skills we'd been taught in the nurse training school. The whole of the sick bay was geared up to the highest standard of care—except for Sam.

Sam Burly was the deputy charge, nicknamed "Flicker "because of his habit of saying flicking instead of actually swearing. From morning to night it was flicking hell, flicking staff, flicking this and flicking that.

Like Bill the Bastard he didn't bother to learn the names of the staff but, being a more social animal than Bill, he called everyone 'Pal'.

The administration had boobed in placing Sam as deputy on a ward which required some nursing skill—especially in a position where he was in charge three days a week. His world was a million light years away from that of the students and he fell the natural butt for many of their practical jokes.

Work in the sick bay was a lot harder than on most of the other wards both physically and mentally. Without the worker patients nurses worked almost non stop from the moment they came on duty. So, taking a rise out of Sam was one way of relieving the pressure.

Classical books were his bete-noir, apparently never having passed much further than the 'Dandy' comic and the 'Racing Times' in his reading.

The first time I encountered Flicker was the day after one of the other students had spoken to him in the office. He was looking worried and muttering to himself. The student had said to him:-

"*If you see a seafaring man with both his deadlights out and walking with a limp—let me know. There'll be a threepenny bit for you at the end of the month if you'll do that small thing for me.*"

Having never read Treasure Island Sam hadn't a clue what was going on. Nevertheless—he kept a look out for the blind man "*just in case.*"

My days were well spent in the sick bay and I learned many practical skills. Suturing cuts, urine testing, insulin injections, and medicine rounds, using a medication cart, caring for patients pre and post operations, nursing a variety of patient illnesses and being involved in Electro Convulsive Therapy (ECT), fracture clinics, various visiting specialist clinics and escorts to local hospitals. Life was varied and never dull.

The charge shared all nursing tasks equally between the available students on duty and made sure we all had our chance at undertaking every nursing task available. Only when Flicker was on duty the student occasionally nurses missed out.

One morning Flicker and I were on-duty in the out-patients clinical room when the telephone rang. It was one of the staff from the seventy nine bed epilepsy ward. (Don't blame me for that name. It was always known as such.)

One of their younger patients had fallen down some stairs during a severe epileptic seizure and the injuries he'd sustained were more than the simple routine suturing task performed by the nurses. His badly lacerated eyes would require stitching by the medical officer. Flicker would normally have left assisting the suturing to one of the students but whenever a doctor was involved the chance to impress and possibly increase the prospect of promotion could not be missed.

He would assist the doctor and I could stay and watch and see how it was done. Of course the hospitals for the mentally handicapped don't have the luxury of central sterile supply and everything is prepared in the wards. Eyeless suture needles were not available and all the needles for stitching had to be sterile threaded using forceps—not such a difficult task once one got used to it.

Flicker asked me to prepare the suture trolley and it was all ready and waiting for the doctor by the time he arrived. Not knowing how many stitches the wound would require I'd prepared five needles of varying sizes and threads. The patient was seated in front of the doctor and was in such a shocked state it was decided not to bother with a local anaesthetic. The wound was jagged round the edges and very close to the eyes.

I was grateful that the doctor had decided to do this one himself and not allocate the job to the nurse. I quietly watched, fascinated as the stitches were painstakingly inserted drawing the edges of the wound together. The doctor needed more needle and thread than I'd made up and he asked his assistant, Flicker, to prepare some more. I stood horror stricken in the corner as he picked up a needle and thread from the sterile trolley with his large unsterile hands.

Fortunately, depending on whether you were the nurse or the patient, the doctor had his back to Flicker and was bent over the patient examining the wound. Flicker caught the end of the suture thread between his lips and taking sight over the top of his glasses, threaded the needle. He clipped this unsterile assembly into a pair of sterile forceps and passed it to the doctor who completed suturing the wound.

Oblivious of the incident. The Doc. washed his hands, made a few notes on the medical card and left the ward.

I wasn't, even though a third year student, confident enough to challenge Flickers technique of threading sterile needles. I was full of remorse and judged myself guilty of complicity in this pathetic treatment.

For the next week I tried to get assigned to the suture out patient clinic each morning. Bad lacerations such as the one this patient had experienced were usually checked daily by sick bay. I watched carefully for any sign of a suture infection—none came. Flickers antiseptic spit hadn't let him down. Nevertheless I breathed a sigh of relief for the patients when threaded suture needles were added to the hospital stock.

Although Halley was called a hospital its medical service was almost non existent. For two thousand five hundred patients we were staffed with only four doctors. Most diagnosis and treatment was done by the nursing staff and confirmed with the doctor over the telephone.

Medical Records were merely a confirmation of actions taken and completed en-mass during a weekly visit.

The hospitals medical team consisted of a Physician Superintendent, his Deputy, old doctor Davids and the local G.P.

The Physician Superintendent was a man before his time. He could see the deprivation, lack of staff and archaic and shoddy care that was going on round about him but seemed powerless to do anything about it. He was being asked to run a hospital on a shoestring budget and with very little support from his management committee.

It is a strange thing about many representatives on institution management committees including those of most hospitals They seem to like the status that goes with the job but lack the stomach for the fight and work hardest at preserving the status quo instead of improving services. Often blindly following the dictates of the Government of the day without questioning whether changes are in the interests of the patients. It is though you have to be a weak person to be appointed to such a post.

Frequently our Physician Superintendent would produce good ideas which would benefit the patients and improve their quality of life only to have his hopes frustrated by a tired and indifferent senior nursing staff.

Out of very necessity he would spend a lot of his time fighting with the managers or the unions, with the administrators for funds or with his colleagues for standards. He was in effect a full time Administrative Officer—one less doctor for the patients.

On to the shoulders of his deputy fell most of the responsibility for the care of the female patients—some twelve hundred women and girls. So, it wasn't surprising that many patients could go for years without having their medication reviewed. When I first started at the hospital, four years earlier, he'd just arrived and was a very energetic man who could often be seen hurrying from ward to ward. Later he lost some of his zip and wandered round the hospital giving a good impression of a man suffering from battle fatigued.

Old doctor David's had long passed the official retirement age but the hospital was having difficulty finding someone to replace him. Slow to the point of being only one step ahead of death, he could just manage to visit a couple of wards a day and then only to write out repeat prescriptions. If any of the patients required a change of drugs he'd send them to sick bay and hope that one of the others would visit them before he had to make a decision.

In effect, the only doctor the male side of the hospital had for long periods was the village G.P. I suspect that the 'real' patients in his practice in the village kept him honest. After all, they'd complain if his treatment wasn't right. The G.P's knowledge was current and he wasn't afraid of modern drugs and their use.

As students we often had the latest information at our fingertips and he was not backward in asking us what we thought of a particular treatment or of sharing his own knowledge with us. We all admired him and he brought an air of sanity into the health care of the residents. It soon became apparent that the care of all fifteen hundred male patients was mostly his responsibility.

After I'd been on the sick bay for a couple of months Dr. Davids suffered a stroke and was forced to retire. At long last a new doctor was to be appointed. The bastions of male supremacy crumpled as our only applicant for the vacancy was a woman.

Thus Dr. Winslow was appointed. She was in her mid thirty's and very attractive especially to a group of people who's major part of any working day was devoid of contact with the opposite sex.

Dr. Winslow had a noticeable effect on both our charge and deputy. Which ever one of them was on duty would spend ten minutes in the office behind locked doors—sprucing themselves up before the doctor came to do a round. The area round the office began to smell more of Old Spice than antiseptic. A mere third year student like me very rarely got a look in—not that I was interested—she was too old—at least 30 something.

About an hour after the doctors round one morning, Sam came rushing down the corridor towards me.

"Eh! Lad," he gasped breathlessly," Doctors left her flicking stethoscope behind. Take it over to the flat for her."

It would make a change to get away from the ward for a few minutes so I readily agreed. The doctors flats were elitist residences situated above the medical administration and as Dr. Winslow was the only resident doctor her quarters would be easy for me to find. I bowled up to the door bearing her name on the second floor of the building and boldly knocked.

"Come in." called a soft feminine voice.

I entered into a spacious lounge to find the doctor out of her uniform white coat. In fact, she was out of most of her clothes, just a slip and a flimsy frilly housecoat was all she was wearing. The coat was one of those with a plunging neckline and gave me a generous view of her ample, creamy white breasts. The air was filled with heady perfume which had the added smell of expense rather than the cheaper versions that most of the student nurses wore.

"I've brought your stethoscope Dr. Winslow." I stretched out my arm with the rather limp artifact dangling from it.

"Thank you." She smiled. "By the way, we're off duty up here and my name is Ann."

She took the stethoscope from my proffered hand and started to walk towards one of the doors leading from the lounge. Then she half turned and with another smile said.

"Sit down for a moment."

Innocent me did as I was bid. I thought she must have a message for me to take back to the ward. Dr. Winslow turned and walked through the door. I could see as she opened it that it was a small kitchen. Gosh. I thought, these doctors have got everything. While I was waiting I surveyed the lounge. It was bright and had those little feminine touches I'd observed in the female nurses home. It was in a stark contrast from the Spartan male quarters. It was quite a big room. Big enough to accommodate any three of the resident nursing staff rooms. One corner had a writing desk and was set up for study. There was an open fire place, three piece suite, small dining area with a table and two chairs, pictures on the wall and wonder of wonders a television set. Lucky bugger, she had her own T.V.

There was a third door leading from the room. That must be to the bedroom. The thought of it raised a little thrill in me. It was just like an apartment in the movies. Dr. Winslow returned but instead of a message she was carrying two large glasses of whiskey.

"I thought you might like a drink." She said, sitting on the arm of my chair and offering a glass. I could feel the warmth of her thighs through the flimsy housecoat pressing against my arm. She leaned forward as she placed the glass in my hands giving me an even more tempting view of those creamy orbs. I suddenly felt very uncomfortable and very hot. This was something out of my league. I grasped the glass in trembling hands, downed the contents in one gulp, and stood up.

"Thank you." I mumbled. "I must return to the ward now we're very busy." I made a hurried exit before anything else could happen.

My last glimpse of the doctor was of her standing by the fire place smiling at me. I didn't mention anything to the lads on the ward. I might have been wrong in what I was thinking. She was, after all, the doctor. With the hectic ward routine and studying the incident soon passed from my mind, although I must confess entered in to my fantasies in the loneliness of my room on the staff block.

After some reflection I dismissed the whole incident as wishful thinking on my part and the need for the only woman doctor in the hospital to have an occasional chat. I put the whole episode behind me until a week later the problem recurred. This time it was the charge who approached me with the doctors wayward patella hammer to be returned. I accepted the task, curious to see what would happen but determined in my resolve to just return the patella hammer and nothing more. I was no virginal youth but—I mean—she was miles older than me.

I must admit that my hopes were dashed as I found Dr. Winslow wearing a day dress and not looking like the seductive siren of my earlier visit to her flat. The perfume and feminism was still there but I no longer felt threatened. This time I took the offered drink and stayed to talk a while. It never occurred to me that drinking early in the day could be an indication of an alcohol problem.

During our chat, I learned she too could be lonely, even with the company of the television, in the quietness of this big flat. Feeling very *"man of the world"* and mature with her scotch inside me I readily accepted her offer to join her for a quiet evening of drinks, T.V. and supper after work.

That night began a very brief and special relationship. I learned from my precious Ann that there is a difference between girls and women and that each have their own delights and pleasures. Ours was a tender and gentle affair from which I learned many things. Our discrete relationship turned an inexperienced youth into a more confident young man, or so I believed. It was not to last though and she was soon transferred to another hospital. Her replacement was another—almost too old to practice—male.

I was reaching the end of my term on sick bay and a spell of night duty was looming up. The hospital put final year students on nights before the examinations and there they remained until after the results came out. We were allowed a week off night duty to attend school just before the examinations but worrying students were better out of the wards and left to their own devices on night duty. With this prospect looming large before me I threw myself into the sick bay routines like mad—determined to make the most of the experience. There were two other students on the ward with me. Dick and Ted. They were determined to make the last days in sick bay as much fun as possible. They became friendly enemies and frequently engaged in battles or practical jokes. One morning they started to argue at seven o clock as we came on duty and were still at it when lunch time came. The war had started at bed making time with pillow throwing and insulting remarks. By lunchtime it had reached the stage where Ted slipped into the staff room and placed a raw egg in Dicks jacket pocket. Just as Dick was leaving the ward to go for his lunch Ted slapped him on the pocket making sure the egg was broken. Dick hadn't discovered the slimy mess until he reached in the pocket for a handkerchief.

Seeking revenge he returned early and entered the ward by the back door. Ted was nowhere in sight but the staff toilet was engaged. Dick was quick to jump at this half chance. He took the fire hose reel from the wall and out through the window into the airing court. Silently he pushed the nozzle through the louvered window of the staff toilet and turned the hose on. The water gushed out by the gallon and a scream as though murder was being committed came from inside the lavatory. Dick dashed back into the ward, leaving the hose running, to watch Teds humiliation. The toilet door flew open and there stood Sam, trousers still round his ankles, white coat rolled up so not to drop in the pan and soaked from head to foot with water still cascading down on him

"Nay! Flicking hell, Pal."

Life was going to be hell in sick bay after this—roll on nights.

Some of the Senior Staff seemed to treat the dispensary at the sick bay as their own personal Pharmacy and usually waited until a student nurse was on duty to amble in and request a couple of Aspirin or Panadol for a headache. Bert even collared me one morning with:

"Gordon lad, 'as Thy any of that Thovaline cream in stock, only I want a bit for the wife 'cos she's a bit sore under her paps."

I managed to keep a straight face while I gave him a jar and trusted his wife's *"paps"* would get better soon.

One further incident occurred while I was rostered on duty in the sick bay which I found hard to come to terms with. I was working in the ward dispensary checking the drugs when Deputy Bill arrived in his usual silent manner.

"Morning Mister." He said.

"Morning Sir,"

"There's a new drug come out for treating anxiety called Librium, have you heard of it?"

Librium had been launched just a few weeks earlier with one of the tabloids showing a picture of a zonked out tiger on the front page and lauding it as a cure—all for most psychiatric ailments.

Keen to show off my up to date knowledge I answered in the affirmative.

"Have we got any in stock?" asked Bill.

We had three residents who were being trialed on Librium and I told him so. Bill asked me to show him some. He took the bottle from me. Extracted and couple of tablets and quick as a flash swallowed them.

"Always pays to have some idea of the effect of stuff you give these people." He said, and left as quickly and silently as he arrived.

I promptly reported his actions to the Charge Nurse who did not seem at all surprised.

"He does that every time a new drug comes out," he said, "Bloody silly if you ask me."

Nothing more was said and nothing further happened about the Librium. It was probably the tip of another of those ice bergs.

Chapter 17

Sports Day

The summer was drawing to a close and so too was my period on sick bay. Night duty, a further study block in school and the final examinations were getting closer and the pressure to achieve was getting serious. One late burst of warmth came to sustain us throughout the winter. It was the sports day.

Throughout the year there was a multiplicity of sports events to keep both patients and staff entertained. We fielded teams at football and cricket to play against other institutions in friendly rivalry and occasional local sports clubs. It was viewed as a welcome bonus to be selected for escort duty on one of the teams away trips. There was a day out of the institution to look forward to and the welcome opportunity to compare your own hospital with another similar establishment. After visiting several hospitals with our team I found that all institutions looked, smelt and acted the same.

This year we were going to go one better than the other hospitals and have an end of season sports day on the main playing field of the hospital.

John Hall, in his capacity as entertainment officer, together with the physical training instructor, was the organiser of this special day.

It was soon evident that this was also going to be an event for scoring promotion points, especially when it was made known the whole of the hospital management committee would visit and view the sports.

There was an abundance of help. Many charge nurses used the occasion to obtain much needed equipment for their patients. For example, new wheelchairs could be obtained for the non-ambulant because it wouldn't do for the management committee to see patients sitting in the old rusty ones. New clothing appeared as if by magic from the charges store, although we wiser staff knew it would return back their just as quickly after the event.

Dave watched all the preparations with amusement.

"It's like the bloody army," he confided. "B-B-B"

"What's that?" I asked although my reason told me I shouldn't.

"Bullshit—Baffles—Brains." laughed Dave, and walked away shaking with laughter at his profound observation. The list of sporting events that circulated the wards was, to say the least, unusual. It was reasoned that the "high grade" young offenders from the refractory wards would win most normal events. John Hall had therefore devised a unique handicapping system. Instead of handicapping the participants he produced a series of events that often had the most able people at the biggest disadvantage. His agile mind came up with such events as; the hundred metre wheelchair race on wet grass; the over sixties race; the slow bicycle race (last one over the line wins), the running backwards race and a sack race with no bottoms in the sacks as *"duds can't jump."*

For weeks beforehand preparations were in evidence throughout the whole of the hospital. The occupational therapy department was turned over almost entirely to making bunting and flags. Electricians couldn't attend to the blown fuses in the wards because they were building a public address system. Carpenters and painters abandoned their routine maintenance tasks to refurbish and redecorate the sports pavilion. In addition they were making a secret project for Mr. Hall in the security of their workshops.

Outings for the residents were all curtailed because the hospital drivers and their transport was diverted to moving chairs and trestle tables, plants from the farm, and running sundry other messages for the sports. Gangs of patients were drafted to work alongside grounds staff on roping out the field, or picking up litter. A huge marquee was erected.

The fateful Saturday eventually arrived. It was a bright warm day and although some clouds were evident on the horizon they didn't seem to pose any threat of rain. This was summer after all.

Early in the morning John Halls secret project was erected on the field. It was a glistening red, white and blue bandstand.

At one o clock the wards started to evacuate and long crocodiles of patients and nurses could be seen streaming their way through the grounds en route to the sports field to get a good vantage point. By two o clock everyone was assembled. Off duty staff had been encourage to bring along their families to swell the crowds and join in the fun.

The new lady chairman of the hospital management committee made the usual introductory speech and declared the sports day open. As soon as she finished speaking there was a racket like hordes of screaming banshees coming from the rear of the pavilion. Heads turned in the direction of the noise as into view came John Hall, marching at the front of his patients kazoo band.

Because very few of the patients possessed the skill to be taught a musical instrument (even if someone had been patient enough to try) John had turned the eurhythmic group into a band. Playing a tune vaguely resembling "Colonel Bogey" they headed towards the resplendent band stand. John at the vanguard stepping high like a marching chorus girl and waving his baton proudly aloft. The band had great difficulty keeping in step and continuing to blow their kazoos but they managed to tag along in cheerful disorder.

They were all dressed in red tunics with large white buttons and shiny epaulettes made out of silver paper. The tunics were fastened at the waist with white cardboard belts and crossed white bandoleers tucked in at the back. They were modified costumes salvaged from one of the hospital pantomimes.

The band would probably have marched and played more in time if it hadn't been for the small man with Down's syndrome bringing up the rear. His was the task of playing the base drum. It was an instrument nearly as big as him. In professional mimic style he'd turned the paper peak of his uniform cap round so that it didn't catch the drum as he walked. Using both drum sticks he was banging hell out of the instrument. It didn't matter to him that he was out of time with the music so long as he made a loud noise.

The impact of the band produced the desired effect and brought an air of festivity to the occasion. The first race was organised and run and the usually vigilant staff began to relax. For once, male and female patients could be seen fraternizing without an overt staff presence. They were walking round the field holding hands, eating ice creams, playing on the side shows which had been constructed for the occasion or just sitting and watching the races. It was becoming a very relaxed and light hearted afternoon. Even the male nurses on duty were able to walk and talk with their female counterparts but at the same time having to keep an eye on their charges and of course look out for Matron.

Towards the end of the sports day the sky began to cloud over making it dull and cool. The races were all run and the crowd slowly began to drift towards the pavilion in anticipation of the prize giving.

Johns little band had played their repertoire of about five tunes manfully all afternoon but were now slowly being isolated in the middle of the field as attention was focused on the pavilion and the committee. This situation somehow didn't appeal to Johns showman instincts and so he ordered his group to pick up the bandstand and carry it nearer to the prize giving area. A few patients who had not yet made their way to the pavilion were drafted in to assist with the move.

The bandstand was lifted in one smooth operation and carried towards the crowd. The sudden cessation of "music" drew attention to their direction.

Then came the only blot on the afternoons proceedings. A couple of more adventurous patients had sought seclusion underneath the band stand and were now uncovered for all to see, half naked and locked in a more than passionate embrace with the flash of the male patients buttocks bouncing up and down in a frenzy. Time seemed to stand still as the couple, so engrossed in their activity, continued oblivious to the loss of the cover of the bandstand. The crowd stood rooted to the spot, not fully believing what they were seeing.

This momentary deadlock was broken by Alf who, for one of his years and weight, strode quickly from the pavilion, placed one foot squarely on the male patients bare rump, pushed down hard and said.

"Gerrout yer dirty bugger."

The young man and woman sprang to their feet and before anyone could stop them dashed, clothes still awry, for the cover of the marquee. A couple of staff discretely followed them and I guessed they'd probably return the offenders to the wards. A few of the senior staff looked embarrassed and flustered but, kindly, the members of the management committee appeared not to notice anything and proceeded with the prize giving as though nothing had happened. Only the staff faces conveyed the witch hunt which would follow in the morning. The Sub Officers gave meaningful looks to a charge nurse. The charge was rolling his eyes in the direction of the staff nurses who in turn grimaced at the student.

The student, who was already hard pressed trying to cope with the thirty patients allocated to him, shrugged his shoulders. He'd take the blame for the patients behaviour as the senior staff all closed ranks.

For most of us, particularly those of us who had no responsibility in the matter, it was just an amusing incident in a very enjoyable day.

Close of Play for the day

Chapter 18

The Refractory

The male patient involved in the affair on the sports field would, as a result of his behaviour, end up for a few weeks on a ward known as the refractory.

The large hospitals for the intellectually disabled/mentally ill are often obliged to cope with an unusual degree of variation in their patients. This frequently means people with borderline intellectual disabilities or violent or severe psychotic and antisocial tendencies were resident in the same facility as those people with more severe intellectual disabilities. Many of the former were detained in the institution from the courts with the operation of a court order restricting their discharge.

Halley hospital had developed separate wards for these patients with the most severe behaviourally disordered people being placed in the ward called the refractory. This forced upon the nursing staff another role. That of confinement and containment—custodial care.

Through common usage the hospital had developed the role of the refractory as a means of control for all inmates who from time to time couldn't be contained in an ordinary ward. Although the ward was called the refractory block by the hospital hierarchy it was openly referred to as the punishment block by grass roots staff and patients. In Halley, patients who too frequently absconded or were openly aggressive and bucked the system were sent to this special ward for a period of 're-training.'

On the refractory a prison-like atmosphere prevailed. Staff were exceptionally cautious when dealing with the violent patients and the higher grade (more intelligent) individuals were encouraged to earn their transfer from this place of restricted privilege by assisting in the containment of the lesser intelligent aggressive group. Life for the patients and staff was tedious.

The basic daily routine consisted of; ablutions followed by cleaning; breakfast followed by cleaning; lunch followed by cleaning; tea followed by cleaning; followed by one hour of recreation and then bed. There was no cinema for these patients, no dances, no social life or outside contacts just cleaning. It was a very clean ward.

For the staff there was very little interaction with the patients other than supervision and service needs like shaving and meals. The whole of their relationship could only be described as one of mutual distrust. The staff spent a lot of their time counting. Counting razor blades, counting bodies, counting keys and the single most important task of counting the cutlery.

"Safe custody of sharp instruments when dealing with violent patients is of the utmost importance."

So the nurses were taught and so the ward practiced.

Hospital legend had it that at one time a patient in a rage had attacked several others and grabbing a bread knife stabbed one person to death before anyone could stop him. Whether this was true or not no one could say but, they weren't taking any chances.

As well as the routine meal time checks, patients beds and clothing were also subjected to frequent spot checks for sharp instruments. It was against this severe custodial background that the event known as the great escape took place.

Six of the more intelligent, aggressive young patients were involved in the escape and it took a lot of ingenuity to organise it.

Meals were taken on the gallery of the refractory ward. That is, the wide corridor area between the dormitory and the day room. This was made possible because the nature of the inmates violent proclivities precluded the admission of more than fifty patients at any one time. This was small for a ward at Halley hospital.

It was necessary to seat all the patients at the same time so that maximum observation could be maintained during the period when knives and forks were in circulation. At meal times the patients were assembled in the gallery. They stood behind their chairs at tables for six and were counted. When all were assembled grace was recited. As on most wards this was adhered to because of the hospital rules rather than any conviction of the staff.

The cutlery wagon was wheeled along the rows of tables and knives, forks and spoons were passed out. They were counted out loudly on a per table basis with the charge marking the number issued to each group on his tally sheet. At the last table the number of implements was called out loud and clear so there could be no doubt in the staff minds of the number issued. When the ward was full the call would be:

"fifty knives, fifty forks, fifty spoons."

As soon as the meal was over the practice was repeated in reverse with the charge crossing off the tables as each one was completed. When all the cutlery was collected up and locked in a wooden box for transfer to the kitchen for washing, staff breathed a sigh of relief and the ward relaxed slightly.

The leader of the escapees was one Ginger Smart. He was more of a recidivist criminal than a retarded person. Sometime in the late forties he'd been committed to the hospital for observation. His criminal career had been non-violent and revolved round breaking open gas meters and telephone coin boxes. So simplistic was his handiwork the police had no difficulty in picking him up after each crime. Especially as he often left signed I.O.U's for the money he had taken.

Following his tenth minor offense the magistrate deemed him to be retarded for getting caught so easily and an order was made to place him in the hospital for observation. Twenty years later we were still observing him.

In part, Ginger had contributed to this situation. He'd learned that by keeping a low profile in the institution his case would be lost amongst the other two thousand inmates. Only those who caused a lot of strife were subject to frequent review. No one can know what his reasons were for wishing to live in the institution—he just did.

For twenty years he'd occupied a position of some trust in the hospital stores. He had a single room in one of the wards and a comfortable, if trifle dreary, lifestyle. There were outings with the hospital groups and even a two weeks holiday at a seaside resort every year as a trusted patient. He could even arrange to have occasional days out with staff members as escort if he wanted them.

Suddenly Ginger's behaviour had changed and he started to abscond. It's reasonable to assume that had he chosen to pursue his discharge in the normal manner he'd have been free of the hospital environment in a matter of weeks. Perhaps it was the challenge of beating the system that got to him and twice he'd run off from working parties only to be brought back by the police a couple of hours later.

After the second absconding he was sent to the refractory ward for a few months to reflect on the error of his ways. The other five who were to escape with him were drawn from the more intelligent and wilder end of the range of handicapped people on the ward.

They were all detained through order of the court for violent offenses. During their meal times the group contrived to remove the screws which supported the sash window behind their dining room seats in the gallery. As the window frames were all painted white, the black hole left when the screws were removed should have been quickly spotted by staff. Ginger and his gang were alert to this one however and had filled the holes up with white soap stolen from the staff washrooms when they were cleaning them.

The ward cleaning was done by the patients with the staff only observing so there was little chance of the window being inspected too closely. How long it took them to do the uncrewing and filling no one knows—sufficient to say it was eventually completed and all that was needed was a sharp knock to remove the window frame.

It was a cold night in November when the group decided to make their move. Three of them slept in the dormitory and the others slept in side rooms off the gallery. Because the hospital was always short of staff only one night nurse was available for the ward. In order to ensure the hospital was secure at night. Each member of night staff was issued with a key which he inserted into several slots in the walls of the ward at hourly intervals throughout the night.

The pegging system as the night staff called it, recorded on a rotating graph attached to a time clock in the sub-officers office. The Night Superintendent could see at a glance if all was well round the hospital wards and if the staff were awake. The use of the keys in several sites on the ward also ensured the night staff left the warmth and comfort of the dormitory fire and walked through the ward at least once and hour.

The pegging slots in the refractory ward were situated one at each end of the big dormitory and one at the end of the gallery. On some of the 'lower grade' wards it wasn't uncommon for the night nurse to give his pegging key to a worker patient so they could peg for him for a few hours while the nurse slept. The patient received the princely sum of twenty Woodbine cigarettes for his trouble at the end of the week. Night staff on the refractory never subscribed to this practice for obvious reasons.

On the night of the escape the three who were sleeping in the dormitory waited until the night nurse went to peg up the gallery on his three am round, and followed him. As he passed Gingers side room he heard Ginger apparently crying. Unlocking the room, thinking he'd nothing to fear from Ginger, he looked in. Quickly his keys were snatched and he was bundled into the side room as Ginger slipped out. The door was closed behind him and as side-rooms can only be opened from the outside the night nurse was effectively trapped.

No one pays any attention to people in side rooms shouting in institutions—that's what they get put into side rooms for.

The remaining two patients were released from their rooms and the escape was on. Up to this point the patients had developed an excellent plan. They even completed the pegging round—so far so good. Why, being in possession of the ward keys, they didn't unlock the door and let everyone out we shall never know?

Why they didn't use the keys to let themselves out is also a mystery?

The weeks of painstaking work on the gallery window must have been uppermost in their minds. That was the route they'd planned and that was the route they were going to take. With a crash they pushed the window free from its surrounds and leapt out.

It was perhaps at this point that the reason for the patients detention in the hospital became apparent. The refractory block was on the third floor of the building. The crash of the window alerted the staff on the floors below they raised the alarm with the Night Superintendent and other night staff. A few from the staff block were quickly on the scene.

What confronted them was a complete shambles.

Three patients were lying on the airing court among the remains of the window frame and shards of broken glass. One had a broken leg, one had a broken ankle and one was lying unconscious. All three were covered in blood from cuts caused by the flying glass. The unconscious patient was later found to have a broken back.

Ginger was picked up by the police in the village waiting at the bus stop for a bus to the city. Of the remaining two escapees. One failed to go out of the window with the others and one was judged to have got clean away. That was, until his body turned up several months later floating in a disused gravel pit. The hospital rules were amended to ensure that staff checked windows regularly.

The refractory was a hard place to work and I was grateful that in all the years I was associated with the hospital I was only asked to work three days on that ward. It was allocated two night staff after that. The only ward that did not need a relief for meals.

Chapter 19

The Funeral

In an institution of the size of Halley death was inevitable. As residents were frail, epileptic or just grew old they died. It was not uncommon for us to have several deaths each month.

I was in the middle of my period of sick bay duty when I was rostered for my first funeral. It was getting towards the end of summer and the weather was starting to turn colder—the nights were drawing in. It was a case of going on duty in the dark of the early morning and returning home in the dark as well. There were many staff who argued this didn't matter because we were always kept in the dark by management anyway.

On sick bay there was little opportunity to take the patients outside and the only daylight we saw in the autumn and winter was through the rain splattered windows or on the way to meal breaks.

Checking the duty roster outside the chiefs office before reporting for work I noticed that I was down to attend a funeral. Up until this time I'd never really paid much attention to this task or even that it existed. There was a tendency to look at the list with an eye out for your own name and then to check the task, so it wasn't surprising that I'd not given this particular duty much thought.

I knocked on the chiefs door and poked my head round. To my relief, Alf was on duty.

"I'm on funeral duty this afternoon sir, what do I do?"

"Well! Gordon lad," Alf smiled. "Just wear full uniform. Smart turn out like. Top coat and gloves if its cold. Then report to Mr. Bentinc at the mortuary for two o clock. The patient was one of those off ward eleven—been here most of his life. You won't start before quarter past anyway. Thee'll be right lad."

With another of his disarming smiles Alf dismissed me.

I left the office non the wiser but at least I knew what to wear and who to see.

I arrived at the mortuary at five to two that afternoon. I was feeling a little happier because Flicker had filled in some of the details.

The hospital owned a small cemetery several miles up the road. It dated back to the days when the hospital was run by the local Asylums board and the inmates were frequently abandoned by their relatives and the outside world once they were admitted. Nowadays it was used for those patients who'd no next of kin or for those who's home was the institution for so many years that their relatives thought it appropriate for them to be buried there.

Several soldiers had also been buried in the cemetery when the hospital had been used by the military during the war. However, theirs was a separate part of the cemetery grounds. Society judged they were too good to be buried alongside the inmates of the institution.

I reported to Mr. Bentinc

"The rells' are coming to this one." He said. "Better put on a show."

Before he could say anything more a funeral car drew up with the funeral director and five people dressed in black sitting rather crushed in the back seat. Following behind with two other men sitting next to the driver was the hearse. The local undertaker immediately recognised Mr. Bentinc and hurried across towards us.

"They want to view the body." He inclined his head towards the relatives and then moving away ushered them in through the mortuary door.

"Take your time." muttered Mr. Bentinc to the retreating undertaker. "I've not got a full team yet."

The small group of mourners passed inside the mortuary doors and out of sight. Mr. Bentinc left me standing by the front door while he moved round the side of the building to grab a last quick cigarette.

Several other staff drifted up. I knew most of them by sight but had never worked with them. They were all nursing assistants who had worked in fixed wards and departments of the hospital for years. Many of them were as ritualistic in their behaviour as the patients and steadfastly resisted change. Funerals were one of their perks. They could always be relied upon to turn up in full uniform and do funerals willingly as it got them away from the ward for a few hours.

I discovered I was only on the detail because one of the regular nurses was sick. There was one kindly faced, white haired older chap whom I recognised because he lived in the nurses home. I smiled a greeting and he must have recognised my nervousness because he came over to talk.

"Relatives here?"

"In there." I indicated the mortuary.

"Know what to do?" He asked.

"No." I confessed apologetically.

"Well," he paused to light a cigarette which he kept well masked in his cupped hands. "We walk either side of the hearse—three on each side. If the relatives weren't here we'd be able to travel in the car. When we get to the burial ground we carry the coffin on our shoulders to the chapel of rest. The minister from the village meets us up there and we have a short service. Then we carry the coffin to the grave and bury 'im. Stay close to me and do as I do and you'll be O.K."

"Thanks." I was much relieved to be given so much help and advice.

My benefactor just smiled and walked over to join the others who had gathered with Mr Bentinc by the door of the mortuary. I tagged along in his wake. The undertaker came out first.

"Ready when you are." he said. Then,

"Watch the driver—he's new."

I didn't grasp the significance of the statement but the rest of the group shot meaningful looks at one another.

We followed the undertaker into the building. The relatives were grouped round the coffin and an attendant was screwing down the lid. One, who I took to be the mother, was sniffing into a handkerchief. They stepped back as we entered the room and created the space for us to line up on either side of the plain wooden casket. There was a single wreath of flowers placed on the lid just below a plain metal plate bearing a name and date.

There was no lifting to do at this stage as the coffin was resting on a small trolley which we propelled towards the door. It was a task which could have been undertaken by just two of us. In fact, the nurse at the rear propelled the trolley and the rest of us just placed our hands on the coffin as a token gesture. The hearse was reversed to the door and the coffin lifted inside. I was surprised at the lightness of it. A second wreath was placed on the top. This was the one from the hospital. The door of the hearse was closed and we lined up on either side of it while the relatives climbed into the car behind.

We set off slowly along the back drive of the hospital grounds. I felt a shiver run down the back of my spine—it seemed like we were participating in some timeless ceremony but without the crowds which should be gathered.

As we neared the barrier which served as a gate to the rear of the grounds, the gatekeeper came out of his 'office'. Standing by the kerbside, he raised the barrier, and pulling himself to attention gave the most magnificent left handed salute. It had to be left handed—it was the only one he had.

Such was the style and precision of this performance that the salute continued until both cars had passed. I was quite overcome by such concern and imagined the tradition was something that started during the war and was a carry over from the hospitals military days. The gateman—from his injuries a returned and wounded soldier—would be remembering his fallen comrades.

Later I discovered he'd lost his arm in a factory accident at the local mill and he just saluted because it gave him something to do while the funeral party passed by.

Once out on the open road the driver of the hearse forgot himself and began to increase speed. It was his usual funeral speed but it became unreasonable when the escort is walking. Our sedate, controlled procession suddenly became a puffing and wheezing group trying to walk at a jogging pace in order to keep up. The breathing was getting heavier and the elderly chap behind me was getting further and further back.

Mr. Bentinc realised the whole thing was about to deteriorate into a shambles and banged hard with the flat of his hand on the side of the car. It made a noise like a shot. The result of this was to make the hearse lurch forward suddenly and then brake hard as the driver was half frightened to death. He wound down his window.

"What's on then?"

"Were not bleeding milers." Gasped Mr. Bentinc, who was as short of breath as the rest of us.

"Go a bit slower."

"Sorry mate." Said the driver apologetically. "I forgot you were there."

We quickly regrouped and continued on our way at a pace more in keeping with the purpose of our duty. The funeral director had sensibly kept the following vehicle some distance behind so the sudden spurt and halt in our progress was largely missed by the relatives.

The finely tuned car purred along and in the still countryside the only sound was the swish of tyres, the crunch of our boots on the tarmac and the laboured breathing of my colleagues. The two and a half mile walk to the cemetery gave me time to reflect on the nature of death. I didn't.

I spent my time examining the revolutions of the rear wheel of the hearse or admiring my uniformed reflection in the high polish of its side panels and generally thinking about what a lark this was away from the ward.

The cemetery was a place of stark contrasts. It was divided into several areas. There was the old soldiers section, Roman Catholics, Church of England and others or Non Conformists. Some of the graves were well tended while others bore only a small headstone without a name—just the patients hospital number. The latter were those who'd died without any traceable relatives. Their only marker that they'd passed through this life was the number which matched a name somewhere in someone's hospital record book.

One very ornate headstone bore the legend:

'The Doctors said our son had the mind of a child of eight. Jesus said 'suffer little children to come unto me . . . . 'It seemed trite. Standing there among all the others.

We bore the coffin on our shoulders into a small purpose built chapel. It was very small and dark inside with the major source of light coming from a small stained glass window above an altar. Someone had erected a wooden trestle on which to place the coffin and we took our places in pews which lined the side of the small church. All the seats faced the aisle and consequently the coffin.

The relatives sat on the opposite side of the church to the staff to form two confronting sets of people looking at one another over the top of a coffin. There was no sign of the minister.

The funeral director paused in the doorway, looked anxiously round the little church and then hurried out again. We heard the sound of a car being started, the engine revving, the slipping of tyres on the gravel drive and then it roared off down the road. Mr. Bentinc whispered to the staff round about him from out of the corner of his mouth.

"Old Pates forgotten again."

The minister of the local church was notorious for his poor memory. Local legend had it that he once dropped his wife off in town shopping while he went and parked the car. Then, while he was trying to find a parking spot, forgot what he was doing and came home without her. He even went to a conference in London by car and then came home on the train. Leaving his car in the hotel car park.

We sat facing the relatives across the small chapel in absolute silence. I wanted to smile at them but, looking at the stony faces of my colleagues, I thought the better of it. After about five minutes Mr. Bentinc got to his feet and in a booming voice announced

"We will sing psalm twenty three."

The rest of the staff stood up and the relatives slowly followed.

"The Lords my shepherd, I'll not want." Mr. Bentinc sang loudly and firmly if not altogether tunefully. The rest of us just tagged along taking our time from him while the relatives came a poor third.

As we got to walking through deaths dark vale a red faced minister followed by an even redder faced funeral director hurried through the door. Mr. Bentinc caught their eyes and with a barely perceptible nod indicated that all was under control. The minister, still adjusting his cassock, took his place and thumbed through his prayer book as we finished singing the psalm. He proceeded with the burial service in the hallowed tone that the clergy seem to reserve for such occasions.

Half way through the service he broke off and walked towards the door. At a nod from Mr. Bentinc we bearers shouldered the coffin and followed him. The wind outside the chapel was quite sharp and caused my eyes to water. There was nothing I could do about it as it was taking both my hands to support the coffin and keep my balance on the rough path of the cemetery. It wasn't until we reached the graveside that I was relieved of my burden and able to find my handkerchief to wipe the tears from my cheeks. Two of the cemetery staff hooked up the coffin and lowered it into the ground.

"Dust to dust, ashes to ashes." The preacher intoned.

We bent and threw earth on to the top of the coffin lid and then the service was over. Mr. Bentinc stood talking to the relatives of the patient at the graveside while the rest of us made our way slowly back to the chapel. We congregated at the door. Silent, no one offering to speak as Mr. Bentinc saw the relatives to their car and watched them drive away.

As he walked back to the group it was as though someone had turned the volume back up. Everyone began to speak. Mr. Bentinc opened his hand and counted out a pound note for each of us.

"From the relatives." He said, "thanks lads."

"Aye—those tears from the young un did it."

"He can come again."

The others, more animated now that the funeral was over were voicing their opinions. Somehow I got the impression that they were pleased with me.

Mr. Bentinc took charge again.

"We can snatch a quick drink at the back door of the pub. Its a long walk back to the hospital."

I could see that this was the regular pattern of funerals and why the team had been a bit reserved at my being there. They were all waiting for Mr. Bentinc's lead with a stranger amongst them.

He'd obviously decided I was all right and that I wouldn't blab to anyone about their perks. I never did, all the time I was at the hospital. Mr. Bentinc must have said something to the subs office though because after that I filled in on several funeral duties when one of the regulars was off sick. I was never 'reduced to tears' again though and we frequently didn't get a reward.

Mr Bentinc always impressed me as the ideal man for being in charge of the funeral detail. He didn't panic and his presence of mind saved more than one sticky situation.

On one occasion the sides of the grave had begun to sag following several days of heavy rain. The coffin was lowered into the ground but only went about eighteen inches in to the hole and then became stuck against the sagging sides. The lid of the coffin was just level with the surface of the ground and despite much juggling and jiggling of ropes by the grounds staff it would not descend any deeper.

Silently and without fuss, arms clasped in front of him, Mr. Bentinc walked to the graveside. Without a word he brought his booted foot down hard on the centre of the coffin lid. This cleared the obstruction and the cask shot down to the bottom of the hole nearly taking the groundsmen with it. Mr. Bentinc, unconcerned, quietly rejoined his group of colleagues. He had the air of one who had done nothing.

He was a man for all funerals.

Chapter 20

Night Duty

At last the time for night duty had arrived. There was no escaping night duty, it was an integral part of the course. It suited the hospital administration to leave our banishment to the night staff as late as possible in our training. With only a small work force for such a large number of patients the policy was to place as few people as possible on night duty. Consequently, it was more appropriate to have senior students on night duty who could take charge of the ward rather than have to double up learners with more experienced staff. The hospital always seemed to be short of staff anyway and with the exception of the sick bay one member of staff per ward was the night duty quota.

My first ward on night duty was the children's ward where I'd frequently worked on days. It was one of the smaller wards in the hospital with only fifty six patients. One night staff was considered sufficient. *'After all there are several worker patients who slept on the ward and they could be woken up to give a hand changing wet beds of incontinent patients if necessary'.*

The hours of duty were the reverse of days. Eight p.m. To seven a.m. although it was always considered reasonable to get to the ward for quarter to eight so the day staff could get off early. Funny how that consideration seldom seemed to work in reverse.

There was no introduction to night duty or a gradual sharing of ward duties with more senior staff until you felt capable of 'flying solo.' It was just a case of report to the ward, receive the, often very brief, report of the days happenings from the charge nurse, collect the drug cupboard keys and you were on your own.

Relief night staff would call to the ward anytime between eleven p.m. and two a.m. To allow a break for meals. The Night Superintendent would visit between nine and ten and again between five and six to receive reports of any unusual incidents.

Each night students had to report to the chief's office before proceeding to the ward. This was to collect the pegging key and check the roster hadn't been changed. The unwritten rules required that I spend some time before going on night duty asking around my colleagues to see what night staff do.

Before the fateful day came I gained two pieces of information.

"Always check the patients are all alive before you accept the keys and take over the ward."

This apparently alluded to an incident several years earlier when the day staff handed over the ward to the night nurse knowing one of the patients had died some half an hour earlier. They'd left his bed untouched to save themselves the onerous duty of laying him out. The night staff would have to report that the patient had died on his shift out of deference to his colleagues.

The other piece of advice was: *"Always use plenty of sheets on a ward of incontinent patients."* That is, either change wet patients as required or change them infrequently but wet some sheets and put them in the linen bags so it looks as if the patients have been changed.

It was with considerable apprehension that I walked on to the children's ward for my first night on duty. I'd collected my key from the Night Superintendent and been told my meal relief was to be at one a.m.

The hand over was given.

"Ev'nin mister."

"Ev'nin." I replied.

"You've 56. 45 In bed and 6 workers watchin' T.V. 10 Workers sleep in the gallery, 5 are just coming back from the cinema. There are 27 E.P's(epileptic patients)—no fits today. Get the ambulants and workers up at six and let the dormitory fire go out by seven. See you int. mornin. G'night."

Before I could reply the charge was off out of the office leaving the ward keys in my hand and telling the day staff they could go. Dammit! My first night handover and I hadn't even checked the patients were all alive.

Not all handovers were taken so quickly. When Joe was on duty there was usually an exchange of pleasantries—discussion about the local football teams chances in the cup. Even some hospital gossip or scandal.

The amount of information about the patients remained constant however. The rule was not to rock the boat. Thanks to the routines established by previous night staff I quickly slid into the night nurse ritual.

The worker patients were a considerable asset and filled in any area I forgot. Being products of the hospital environment they'd adapted a way of getting things done without upsetting the nurse patient relationship and making the staff feel threatened. Routine tasks which nurses should have been organising and weren't were quickly spotted. Information was never given direct in case the staff saw it as a challenge to their authority. Such remarks as:

"Shall I bring the report book down for you nurse?"

"Shall I get the backs trolley ready for you nurse?"

Were all effective ways of reminding the nursing staff of the ward routines in a non-threatening manner. In this way the patients preserved the nurses status and still ensured their own security by seeing the routines and rituals of the ward were not disturbed.

For two weeks I worked on nights on the children's ward. There were no mishaps and I quickly slipped into routine. Long hours were spent sitting at a desk in the dormitory between rounds of changing the incontinent patients. I learned to bring my books on duty with me. The finals would soon be upon us and being on nights gave a lot of opportunity to study

Some of the more permanent night staff arranged their ward in such a manner that, with the worker patients watching out for them, they could sleep for long periods. In this way they were able to work an afternoon shift in a factory or on a building site to supplement their income.

My first ward change was to provide me with my first traumatic experience on night duty. I was asked to relieve on a ward of some seventy severely retarded/intellectually disabled patients. Most of them were young adults and the ward included the usual complement of 10 worker patients. I was the sole night nurse.

The hand over was taken as usual with the exception that one of the worker patients was sick in his room and required medication with plenty of water at two a.m. By ten, the last of the patients was in bed with the exception of two worker patients who were making some tea and toast in the kitchen. It was a standard practice for the more responsible workers to make supper for themselves and the night nurse. They would sit in the dormitory with the night staff for an hour or so before retiring and play cards or share a yarn.

It was a cold night and so I banked up the fire and covered a small table with a clean sheet. I'd pinched the angle poise lamp from the charges office so I could read my books without disturbing the whole dormitory. The patients joined me and we talked about our expectations for Christmas. Then, they went to bed while I settled down with the mental health act for company.

My meal relief came early at half past twelve and I went off to the staff dining room for a bite to eat. When I returned an hour later I woke my relief up and sent him on his way to relieve another ward.

"Nothings happened." He said. "One of them went to the loo in the bottom dormitory but that's all."

I looked along the ward in the direction of the beds in the far end of the dormitory. There was a body in each one and they all appeared to be sleeping. My relief left and I settled back into my chair. It was bitterly cold out and snow was just beginning to fall. I didn't envy him trudging from ward to ward along the hospitals exposed corridors.

Picking up my book I started to read and then paused to check the clock. I had half an hour before the next pegging round and I'd give the medication to the sick patient at the same time. I became engrossed in my reading again and had been hard at work for some fifteen minutes when a movement attracted my attention at the bottom end of the dormitory.

Giving my eyes chance to adjust to the gloom I saw it was one of the less able patients. He was standing in the centre of the dormitory clutching the front of his night shirt. Probably wants the toilet I thought. Well I can take him, do the pegging round and give the pills.

I put my book to one side and picking up the keys off the table made my way towards him. The flickering light from the fire was reflecting off the highly polished floor and I'd no difficulty seeing clearly even away from the brightly lit desk area. As I approached the patient I was conscious of the sound of water splashing and a cold shock suddenly hit my feet. Looking down I found I was standing in a puddle of water.

My immediate reaction was to think the patient had urinated on the floor. As I took stock and saw the extent of the pool I realised this was impossible. There was too much. I could hear a distant sound of running water and followed its direction to the toilets in the middle of the dormitory.

As I opened the door and switched on the light I saw the cause of the trouble. A sheet had been stuffed down the lavatory pan and the toilet flushed. On its own this wouldn't have presented a problem but the ball cock had stuck open and the toilet just kept on flushing.

I jumped on the lavatory seat and turned off the stop valve. The water was freezing. No wonder the patient stopped dead when he felt it round his feet. I led the patient back to his bed. Quickly pegged the walls and went to get a mop and bucket from the sluice.

After a couple of minutes mopping I realised I'd no idea of the extent of the pool of water except that I wasn't making much impression. There was nothing else for it but to turn on the dormitory lights.

As the harsh fluorescent tubes flickered into life I saw that the whole dormitory was about half-an-inch deep in water. It must have been running for ages. The mop and bucket was having very little effect and I was getting nowhere fast. The patients in the dormitory were beginning to stir and I realised I had to do something quickly.

I ran along the gallery and woke up several of the worker patients to come and give a hand. Sleepily they followed me down to the sopping wet floor. Even with several mops and buckets we made very little headway. In desperation I grabbed some sheets off the linen trolley and started to mop with them. That did the trick.

Two at a time we mopped with sheets, wrung them out over the bathtub and discarded them in the linen bag. Slowly the tide receded.

It took us a further half an hour to complete the task and used up nearly fifty sheets. To make matters worse the cold water had reacted with the highly wax polished floor and wood, which was usually a deep rich brown, was now a milky white. It would take a lot of work to return it to its original state.

I looked at my watch. Three o clock and I still hadn't given those tablets. I sent the workers back to bed. Pegged the bloody walls again and hurried to the office. I got the medication from the drug cupboard and unlocked the kitchen to get a glass of water to go with them. The cold water tap wouldn't work. Dammit! Too much water in the dormitory and a frozen pipe in the kitchen. I took some milk out of the fridge. That would have to do.

According to the regulations I should have locked the kitchen door behind me but, I was in a hurry and only going down the corridor after all.

The sick patient was sound asleep. His temperature had been down for a couple of days and the antibiotic medication was just the tail end of his course of treatment so I didn't feel bad about being an hour late with it. He woke just long enough to pop the pills in his mouth, wash them down with the milk, mumble his thanks and fall back asleep again.

Feeling more relaxed after the last hectic hour or so I walked back to the kitchen taking the time to check in all the single rooms that the worker patients had got to sleep again. I thought a cup of tea would be in order and then I'd change some wet beds and write my night report. As I opened the door to the kitchen my eyes nearly popped out of my head.

One of the severely intellectually disabled and hyperactive teenagers had followed me along the corridor and must have entered the unlocked kitchen while I was in the sideroom.

I stood transfixed in the doorway as my eyes traversed the room. All the cupboard doors were open. Torn paper littered the floor whilst in the middle of the room was the patient. He was crouched astride a heap of mangled and torn food.

There were several loaves of bread, wheatabix, cornflakes, eggs, some broken and some not and butter. They were all mixed in a huge messy pile. He looked at me with a wild haunted stare and then, as if realising I was angry and about to put an end to his activities, started to cram food from the heap on the floor into his mouth.

The smell of faeces filled the air. In his excitement the patient had opened his bowels on top of the mound of food and also urinated all over the floor.

In his hyperactive state he had then trampled through the excreta leaving a trail spread over the floor, food and cupboard doors.

Three years earlier, following the example of my peers, I would probably have reacted violently and given the patient a hiding. Now, I just stood and surveyed the scene, taking it all in and trying to formulate a plan of action.

It was hard not to be sick from the smell and the realisation that the patient was feasting from the mess indiscriminately. I closed the door and locked it behind me. I was confident about leaving the patient in the kitchen. He couldn't do much more damage as all the other cupboards were locked and the gas was turned of at the main.

Hurrying back to the dormitory I went into the bathroom and turned both taps on. Only the hot one worked I'd turned the cold one off at the cistern in the lavatory. I quickly turned it back on. Nothing happened. Somehow turning off the water had allowed it to freeze in the pipes.

The hot water was pouring into the bath at a scalding temperature. I turned it off and hurried to the bathrooms on the gallery. No cold water there either. It was nearly four o clock so I pegged again to keep the chief happy and telephoned the ward downstairs.

They had cold water. Down the stairs I raced and collected two buckets full. Three times I made the journey until I'd sufficient water to bath my patient.

The next problem was how to get him to the bathroom without trailing faeces halfway through the ward. Eventually I bundled him onto a sheet and dragged sheet and patient to the bathroom. He thought that was fun and wanted to do it again. It was five o clock before I had finished with the patient and put him to bed and a further half hour and more trips for cold water before I finished cleaning up the kitchen.

Then it was back to the floor below to fill up a kettle and some pans of cold water so the staff and patients could have tea at breakfast.

I wrote my report as briefly as possible trying to explain the events of the night.

It was quarter past six before I got round to waking up the worker patients and we started the round of dressing and changing wet beds. We'd just changed the last patient when the day staff started to arrive. The charge nurse walked on to the ward and straight into his office. I followed intending to give him a blow by blow report of the events of the night. As I walked into his office he turned from his desk and looked at me.

"Your a bit slack Mister." he said accusingly. "You've left the dormitory fire in."

That was it—the last straw. I marched from his office into the kitchen and grabbed one of the pots of water off the stove.

Much to the amazement of my colleagues arriving for the day shift I walked into the dormitory and poured the contents over the fire. There was a great hissing and spluttering as the cold water hit the hot coals. Clouds of steam and sooty smoke poured from the fireplace and quickly enveloped the dormitory in a thick fog.

I stormed back into the kitchen and dropped the pan into the sink with a clatter.

"The rest of my report is as written." I yelled angrily at the charge nurse and throwing the ward keys onto his desk hurried from the ward. Slamming the door behind me.

I handed in my pegging key at the office and went to the dining room where my anger carried me through breakfast and up to my room. Once in bed the enormity of my petulant behaviour hit me. I experienced very little sleep knowing I would have to face the music when I reported for duty that evening. I had a horrible sinking feeling in the pit of my stomach as though I'd eaten a lead weight.

I reported for duty early hoping that my telling off would soon be over with. The Night Superintendent said nothing about the incident just handed me a pegging key and told me.

"Same ward as last night."

No telling off, no threats, no nothing. I hung about the corridors until half past seven and then ventured to the ward. As I walked into the office the charge nurse grinned at me.

"That was some night you had last night lad. I read your report and the workers told me the rest. I hope you have it easier tonight. there's no changes."

The charge handed me the keys to the ward and left. He suddenly became the best charge nurse in the hospital as far as I was concerned and for the rest of my nights on his ward I worked my hardest to do the job as he would have liked it done.

As I neared the end of my stint on night duty. I was sent to work for a week to gain night experience in sick bay. It was the only ward in the hospital allowed two night staff (although two were awarded most nights to the refractory following the "Great Escape."), one of whom must always be a trained nurse. The staff nurse I was rostered to work with was Ted Fry.

Ted had a lot of family connections in the hospital as did many of the staff. His father was a charge nurse, his mother worked in the occupational therapy department, his younger brother, Ben, had just started as a student nurse and his cousin worked in the kitchens. It is not uncommon for hospitals in rural areas to employ several members of the same family. This had a very positive side to it by encouraging a family atmosphere and a strong sense of loyalty to the establishment. However, the disadvantages occasionally outweighed the positive attributes.

- Off duty rosters would be designed around family needs and not round the needs of the patients.
- Family communication groups conveyed information, sometimes wrongly, faster than jungle drums.
- The same supportive families could band together against the hospital exerting unreasonable pressure groups.
- Favouritism for key positions and tasks was rife.
- Promotions were not always based on skills and ability but on which person to whom the candidate was related.
- Change was vigorously resisted especially if it threatened the families perceived stability.
- Discipline of severe misconduct was almost impossible as the family influence could extract a vow of silence from most witnesses.

Strangely enough the greatest users of the family power base were the union officials. One senior shop steward managed to find *"cushy numbers"* for all of his family including his cousins and in laws.

Ted had managed to break with this conformity in some part by steadfastly refusing to live with his family on the hospital estate. He'd even gone so far as to refuse the offer of a hospital house when he got married and was buying a house in the village. They'd one child and he further angered the family by not letting his wife work part-time at the hospital agreeing that she stayed at home with the baby. His reward for this non-conformity was a permanent night duty shift in the sick bay. A sort of ostracism by isolation.

Ted was a tall thin individual well over six feet which made him look much thinner. Like many people who worked on the night shift his skin was pale and the blue shadow from his beard and slightly stooped shoulders he gave the gaunt impression of someone who was wasting away from malnutrition. He wore his jet black hair clipped short in military fashion and sported thick-rimmed black spectacles half way down his rather prominent beaky nose. His mouth seemed set firm and severe as though everything in the world was serious.

In direct contrast to his appearance he was full of energy and vitality with probably the most advanced sense of humour in the whole institution. He used his physical appearance and unsmiling features to the utmost, often sending students on the most outrageous of errands.

He once stopped Mark Holden, a West Indian pre PTS student, on the corridor leading to the wards and told him there was an emergency in the sick-bay and would he run and get the sterile fallopian tube from the dispensary and bring it to the ward. As if to add haste to the request he bustled off in the opposite direction.

First year nurses didn't argue with senior staff nurses and Mark's knowledge of female anatomy was not very good. (They did not study anatomy until the end of PTS). He raced to the service window of the dispensary and rang the bell urgently. Hospital pharmacists are not easily phased by events. So when Halley hospital's pharmacist was greeted by a panting West Indian demanding a sterile fallopian tube he quick wittedly masked his smile and directed Mark to the Matron because *"he didn't have one. But he knew Matron did"*

Mark was new to the hospital and even if he'd heard of 'Hell fire Harriet' his mission of mercy transcended all other considerations. Straight through the locked doors which separated the male from the female side of the hospital he hurried and banged loudly on Matrons office door.

"Come."

The "in" was unnecessary in Matrons view. Mark was fortunate, or unfortunate depending on your point of view, finding Matron in her office so late in the day. We can only imagine what must have happened when she looked up from her desk towards the door to see the breathless frame of a large, black, West Indian male nurse asking the question.

"Please Matron, have you got a sterile fallopian tube?" According to Mark. Matron treated him kindly and informed him quite firmly that: *"She did have two in fact but that they were both in use."* He also suggested she smiled, but we found that a bit hard to believe. She gave him an anatomy text book and made him sit down outside her office until he had found one.

On another occasion Ted sent two very new nursing assistants on a round tour of the wards carrying a Thomas splint and the question: *"Have you got a leg to fit this for the sick bay?"*

My first encounter with Ted's sense of humour was when he looked me up in the dining room before we went on duty for our first night together. I was sitting with and Irish student called Terry. He was in the group following mine and true to tradition was trying to find out what happened on nights. I was now an 'experienced' night nurse and was expounding the philosophy of the night staff to my eager audience, as Ted joined in.

"There is nothing to it once you've got your routines established." I was saying.

"That depends what ward you're on." Ted joined in the conversation.

"What do you mean?" Terry asked the question.

I was all ears as well. My experience of night duty was after all limited to two wards.

"Well, What ward are you on?" Ted was directing his question towards Terry.

"Ward 2. The ward above ours." I answered Terry's question for him.

"Oh! Dear," exclaimed Ted looking shocked. "And your first night too."

He sat quietly staring at his cup of tea and slowly stirring it with a silent spoon. Terry and I were not going to be denied.

"What about the ward."

"Go on, you've started now."

"Yes, you must tell us if its something we should know."

Reluctantly and after much cajoling and oaths of secrecy on our part Ted decided to enlarge on his theme.

"Well, it goes back to the war years. As you know from the history of the hospital certain wards were turned over to the army during the war. Ward 2 was one of them. One evening two of the patients started to argue over a woman and the noise that followed soon had the whole ward in an uproar. A big sergeant orderly heard all the fuss and came to investigate. In his effort to separate the two men he pushed one backwards through the window and killed him.

Of course he was acquitted of any charges and that was the end of that, but for one thing. The two soldiers were fighting over whether the wife of one of them was having an affair. The men were in fact friends and the row had started because one of them passed on the rumour to his mate that his wife had been seen frequently with another man while he was in hospital. The chap who died was the married one and his wife was having an affair—with the sergeant who helped him through the window."

Ted paused for effect as he delivered the last line of his narrative.

"What's that got to do with working on Ward 2 at nights." I asked.

"Nothing." said Ted.

Then after another dramatic pause.

"Except that there are staff in the hospital who swear the ghost of the dead man returns from time to time and tries to climb through the window to extract revenge on the sergeant."

A glance at Terry showed that the bolt had got home. He was a very superstitious and impressionable young Irishman who'd been brought up in a small country village where tales of the supernatural and ghosts were commonplace. He was sitting wide eyed and open mouthed giving Ted his full attention.

Ted took out his pipe and leisurely filled it. Then, leaning forward to pick up the matches lying by my packet of cigarettes on the table he lit up. Slowly drawing deep gulps of aromatic smoke into his mouth and not putting the match out until the top of the pipe was fully aglow, he settled back in his chair. Terry and I were beside ourselves at this long silence. Suddenly Ted spoke.

"What date is it?"

"Tenth of October." said Terry.

"Yes." Said Ted, thoughtfully puffing away. "It's about this time of the year the ghost appears."

Then before anything more could be said on the subject he quickly stood up and addressed me

"Cummon Gordon, time to be on the ward."

Ted made no further conversation on the way to the ward just sucked on his pipe and hummed a little Irish jig to himself. We paused at the ward door while I fumbled with my keys and Ted knocked the smoking embers from his pipe on the corridor rail. Then we were inside the brightly lit ward and taking the report. Aside from his humour, Ted was also a first class nurse of sick people and there was no further conversation other than those dialogues of a strictly professional nature whilst we attended to the needs of those in our care.

There were diabetic suppers and insulin injections to give, urines to test, drugs to give out, intravenous infusions to change, antibiotic injections to give, observations to make, backs to be rubbed and patients turned, bed pans, bottles and toilets.

A patient with severe epilepsy was brought to the out-patients to have a cut to his chin treated and Ted took the opportunity to revise me in suturing technique. He even let me put the last few stitches in. It was midnight before we were clear enough of work to grab a cup of tea. By this time, most of the patients had settled and the pace had slackened. I used the opportunity to return to the theme of the dining room.

"Was there really a murder done upstairs?" I asked.

"Buggered if I know." said Ted "But, Irish seems to think so—and he'll think so even more before the nights out."

Just then the night relief arrived and I was sent off duty for my meal break. Ted's wife prepared sandwiches for him and he preferred to take his break on the ward and eat them in the office. This was frowned on by the night supervisor in other wards but it suited him in Teds case because he was the only other trained person on nights and the night super would have had to do the relieving.

Back in the dining room I met up with Terry. He was on first meal break and was just about to go back to his ward. No—he hadn't seen any ghost—but he had asked the charge about the murder and he'd verified the story as correct. Then he had to go. I ate a thoughtful meal. If the charge on 2 said the story was correct. Then why had Ted said he didn't know.

It did not occur to me that the solidarity of the trained staff was such that it would extend to confirmation of such an odd tale to a student. When I returned to the ward and my night relief had left. Ted suddenly came to life and briskly disappeared to the sluice room only to reappear a few minutes later with a foam rubber pillow tied to a broom stave. The pillow was dressed in a patients night shirt and a face had been penciled on to its front.

"Meet the ghost of Ward 2" He said.

Ted unlocked the door which led to the ward verandah and I followed him out into the cold night air.

"Hold this." he said, passing me the 'ghost' and with an amazing show of agility and strength for such a fragile looking individual he shinned up the drainpipe and swung himself on to the verandah roof. I passed up the effigy on a stick and watched as Ted inched up the sloping glass roof until he was lying just below the dormitory window of the ward above. Then, swinging the broomstick in an arch he began to tap the windows of the ward above with his 'ghost'. For a few minutes nothing happened.

Suddenly there was a scream from the ward above which could have heralded the day of judgment. Certainly it would have been heard in Ireland. At the sound, which I was convinced should have woken the whole hospital, Ted pulled the broomstick towards himself and crouched low below the window.

"Anything." He whispered.

"Nothing." I replied. I looked up at the now silent ward above. Ted threw me the broom and then slid down the roof and swung down to the airing court beside me. He grinned.

"I bet that gives Irish something to think about." He said. "Well, back to work."

The rest of the night, even though we worked harder than on most wards, seemed to drag for me. I wanted to get down to the dining room for breakfast to hear from Terry about the ghost. Ted would go straight home after the shift. For him the essence of the joke was in its preparation and execution.

Finally, the day staff arrived. Ted gave me the pegging key (yes, even on the sick bay) and let me go off duty. I ran down the corridors, handed in the key to the super and waited expectantly for Terry in the dining room. He arrived a couple of minutes after me, grabbed a plate of the tacky glue which passed as an apology for porridge and came across to join me. His face was flushed with excitement.

"It came—I saw it." Terry flopped into the chair opposite and leaned forward, his eyes glistening bright and cheeks slightly redder than usual.

"Saw what?" I had decided to play it cool.

"The ghost!" Terry exploded. "It came—just like Ted said."

"Go on,"

I was warming to the situation now. Terry launched into his tale.

"It was after our meal break—about one o clock. I wasn't very busy and was reading a book. I'd decided they were having me on. Then there was this tapping on the window. It didn't register at first. At home we had trees all round the house and so it was a noise I was used to. Anyway, I looked up and there it was."

Terry was filled with the subject now and needed no encouragement from me to continue.

"The ghost was the man who was killed. He was wearing a patients night shirt and trying to get in the window."

My stomach was aching from trying to suppress my laughter and look amazed at the same time.

"What did you do?" I asked, trying to appear enthralled.

"Bloody ran for it—what else." said Terry.

"I locked myself in the loo for half and hour until I had to come out and peg the clock. Thank God it had gone or I don't know what I'd have done."

"You had a narrow escape." I agreed "What next?"

"I think I'll ask the chief for a transfer from Ward 2" lamented Terry. "But I don't know what excuse I can give."

"Well, I wouldn't tell him about the ghost." I advised.

"No fear—he wouldn't believe me anyway." Said Terry.

"No—probably not." I consoled and then making some lame excuse left the table and hurried from the room before I burst with the laughter building up inside me.

After a very rewarding week with Ted I had one more night to work and then it was back to days and ready for the finals. Several staff were off sick when I reported for duty and I was taken to one side by the Night Superintendent as I called to collect the pegging key.

"Sorry to drop this on you on your last night." he said. I instinctively stiffened. This approach usually heralded bad news. Thoughts raced through my mind in anticipation of what was coming next. They were leaving me on nights for a bit longer. He wanted me to work on the refractory. These and a myriad other possibilities added to my unease. But, I wasn't prepared for what was coming next.

"We're very short of staff and I wondered if you could manage Ward 8 and Ward 9 for the night." he continued. "Even if its only until we can find someone to work."

The enormity of what he was saying percolated through my nervous worries. Ward 8, had eighty young to middle aged patients all with severe epilepsy. It was the ward of the chain gang. Ward 9, had over a hundred moderately intellectually disabled/ personality disordered people in residence all in their early to mid twenties.

They were both locked wards and the ward 9 people were only known to me by sight from cinema and dancing groups. I knew that on Ward 8 alone seventy patients slept in one huge dormitory either side of the ward corridor. Two rows of beds along each side and separated by a row of supporting columns and arches. The beds were placed about 12 inches apart and were only six inches off the floor in case a patient fell out of bed during a seizure.

Many of the patients were incontinent and needed changing during the night and with such a bed arrangement it was a full time task in itself. In addition, my experience on days told me to expect some bizarre behaviours and several severe seizures. The superintendents voice continued cutting through my thoughts.

"Of course it may be just for a couple of hours—but be prepared for it to be all night. You could take the reports and then stay on ward 9. because they don't go to bed until half past nine. The patients in ward 8 will all be in bed except the workers and you could get one of them to sit in the dormitory. Then all you need to do is bob down stairs from time to time to check on things. What do you think? Can you manage?"

Even after four years in the hospital I was still in awe of the senior nursing officers and felt completely lost. If I said no—then I may be damning my future employment prospects and judged incapable of taking responsibility. If I said yes—then I was taking on a task which was impossible and would probably make a hash of it.

It was catch 22 and quite insane.

The fates saved me from having to make the decision as one of the students was brought into the office by Alf. He'd been accosted making his way along the corridor for an evening out.

"This young fella volunteered to work tonight." Said Alf, giving the student a hard look which said you'd better agree.

"We'll give him the day off tomorrow." continued Alf benevolently, knowing full well that the poor student would spend most of the next day in his bed sleeping.

"Oh!" I said, quick to seize the opportunity," in that case I'll just do ward 8"

Better the devil you know.

The supervisor gave me the pegging key and I did a quick retreat from the office just in case anyone else telephoned in sick. If there was a double ward to look after I would rather it not be me.

Just as I finished night duty I was called to the Chiefs office. It seemed that jumping John Hall had another brainwave. The nearby town was having a festival complete with a procession of floats along the main street. He had suggested that, due to the shortage of staff, we should promote the Hospital by manning a float.

It seems I had drawn the short straw and along with another student colleague was to help man the float.

Thus it was, I became for the day, the famous Dr Livingstone, riding on a float which proclaimed "*Good Nursing Lights the way to Good Mental Health.*"

I reluctantly did as I was bid.

There was an up-side however, lunch at the local pub, free beer and a few town girls who are a suckers for a uniform.

The Author as Dr Livingstone—doing his bit for recruitment

Chapter 21

The Finals

At last the night duty term was over and I was instructed to report to the school of nursing for the final revision block. The group of twenty students who started was now down to 4. Two males and two females. The equality of numbers had been preserved by happy accident as I was the only original member of the group. The hospital called this loss of students attrition. Most staff called it a bloody waste.

Some of the group still worked in the hospital as assistants having lost interest in training, some found the study too hard on top of full time employment but most had just left—defeated by the system. Even my own dear Margaret had left to try her luck at "real nursing" in the general hospital. The other male nurse was a student who'd failed the last finals and was re-sitting. The two females were post graduate general nurses who'd joined the course during the year.

This proved quite a stroke of luck as the finals were to be taken in a hospital in the major city some 40 miles away.

For the practical part of the examination we'd still be examined in pairs and if we had an odd number of candidates one of us would have been paired with a stranger from another hospital. I believe we had an added advantage in working with the girls who were already general trained as they had a great deal of practical experience in their favour when it came to bed side nursing.

Big John was still in charge and because we were such a small group knew all our strengths and weaknesses. He'd arranged a schedule of individual tutorials as well as group discussions. Boy had we grown up from those early days. Things which had held great fears for us were now no longer problems. Anatomy and the bones of the skeleton were like familiar friends. Physiology and the bodies systems were no longer mysterious but exciting and challenging. An oh! The brain—will we ever totally understand it in all its subtleties. Strategies for teaching and training the intellectually handicapped patients were dissected and tested against reality. We recited the Mental Health Act and then translated it into plain English.

How did we cope with violence? There was still a tendency to use drugs a lot, but, skills were emerging with our experience. We'd learned how to take the heat out of many situations which previously ended in violence.

We looked at our future role as service providers and the slow nature of change within the institution. Sadly we came to the conclusion the nature of the institution prohibited it helping the people it was there to serve.

It was a very exciting time. As the finals were to be taken so far away from the hospital and no accommodation could be provided for us to stay overnight we managed, with big John's help to get the institution to provide us with a car and driver.

There was to be one full day of written papers and the practical of an hour and half would be two days later. The group resolved we'd not take a drink between the examinations but reserve ourselves for a big blast when it was all over.

Big John set us the internal hospital finals. Such was the network of personal knowledge between Matrons and Schools of Nursing that prospective employers would often ask how you went in your hospital examinations rather than whether you'd passed the state finals. The hospital examination certainly introduced us to the pressure of finals and with perfect timing big John gave us the result that we'd passed on the day before we set off for the states.

The state examinations came and went in a blur of frantic activity. Getting up early, driving to the city. Waiting, writing, holding post mortems on the paper, writing some more. *Good God, does that candidate want more paper*—I'm only half way through my answer book. A pause. Then, off again to get through the practical.

"Wasn't that Matron a bitch. Hellfire Harriet was an angel compared to her. Did she ask you the one about . . . . ?."

The finals were over. Three years work done. All we could do now was wait, and wait and wait. One of the worst tortures ever invented is the wait after examinations. The problem is added to if the environment you work in keeps holding out constant reminders of what might be.

Many thoughts flicker through your mind at this time. *'If I fail I'll just take the examination again.' 'If I fail, I couldn't face everyone so I'll just leave.'*

This latter feeling is so strong that many students do leave the service and request the results be posted on to them. Its a time of Limbo and uncertainty. *'If I pass then I won't let it change me—I'll not join their clique. 'If I pass I'll be one of the senior staff and boy will I give those students and assistants hell.'*

It's a time of paradoxical feelings with moods changing by the hour. Finalist's must be of very little use to the hospital during this time of limbo. In my case the wheel turned the full circle and I found myself back on the children's ward.

On this occasion though, I was no mere youngster trying to please. Joe's deputy was off sick and the staff nurse was on annual leave. That left me as the acting, unpaid, deputy.

The winds of change were beginning to blow through the hospital as the new mental health act began to bite. Horror of Horrors we changed the classification titles of our patients from Idiots, Imbeciles, feeble minded and moral defective. to Severely Subnormal, Subnormal, and Psychopathic Disorders.

Not that any of this mattered to the patients or staff of Halley. Patients were still duds, high grade and ward workers. Wards which had remained unchanged for years suddenly were too big and the pressure was on to 'grow smaller.'

The rear guard of senior staff were fighting battles on every front to preserve the total institution and every gain for the patients carved out on this battlefield had a cost. Sometimes it was a situation of residents being encouraged to leave the hospital environment before they were ready and flounder in a society which had already rejected them. They got lost with the derro's and the drunks and finally ended up in some other institution like prison.

At other times it was overprotection by the staff, clinging to their clients apron strings in an effort to save them from the big bad world. Wards that were suffering most were those with a high level of dependence on worker patients to get through the daily household routines.

The experts and planners who'd orchestrated the exodus hadn't taken into account the valuable service these workers provided. As they left the hospital, in many cases to take their rightful place in society, there were no pairs of hands, patients or staff, to replace them and fill in the gaps.

New patients were admitted, so we didn't grow smaller because the need for beds was still there. Those who did come in had more severe intellectual disabilities or more complex behaviour disorders. It was a case of a system trying to provide higher levels of care with fewer and fewer resources.

Programmes which had started to flourish as the new enlightened training caught on, began to die as the manpower resource was unable to meet the need.

The enormity of this problem was brought home to me on my second morning back on the children's ward. The numbers and mix of children remained the same. Fifty six patients of many and varied levels of ability. The worker patient population had reduced to five—and the five least able at that. I looked at my team of staff to work the thirteen hour shift. I had myself, not quite trained, a second year student nurse, and two Italian nursing assistants.

I sent the student down to the dormitory to look after the patients with severe physical problems and asked the nurse assistants to look after the children in the day room by firstly attending to their personal hygiene. The reply of my 'new assistants' rocked me. "Please—No speaka da Inglis."—Nothing had changed.

For the rest of the day I totally exhausted my acting powers as I mimed to these new staff, all the routine tasks that nurses of the mentally ill and intellectually disabled are required to perform. How were the children ever going to speak English if the nurses couldn't.

Slowly, like some great beached whale inching itself towards the sea, the institution began to lurch forward into a progressive new era. But—it was not going to change overnight and no one, even to this day, would like to own up to the way the uniform was to be abolished on the male side of the hospital.

When I first joined Halley hospital there was a standard uniform for all the male nursing staff. It consisted of a three piece navy suit similar to that worn by petty officers in the navy, white shirt, black tie, black socks and shoes or boots, and a peaked cap. The jacket buttons were mat black and I was amazed to see embossed on mine the words 'Lunatic Asylums Board.' Charge nurses had a broad pale blue ring round the bottom of their jacket sleeves, seconds or deputies had two narrow bands and staff nurses one narrow one. Students and assistant nurses apparently didn't count and had nothing. The uniform used to cause me considerable embarrassment whenever I wore it outside the hospital because one local lady used to confuse me with the gas man. I was often hailed in the street with: *"When are you coming to read our meter?"*

The chief, deputy and assistant chiefs all wore a smarter uniform than the rest of us. They looked like police officers with waisted jackets and braid on their caps. The Chief Male Nurse had his three silver pips on the shoulders of his jacket, the deputy two and the assistants one. The ex-servicemen on the staff developed many strategies for keeping their uniform in good condition including sewing the creases in their trousers—it was more effective than modern perma-press.

In these changing times, it entered someone's head that the people who had mental disorders or were intellectually handicapped are not sick in the physically ill sort of way. Nor are they all criminals even though some of them had committed crimes and came to us through the courts. Uniforms which resembled those of the prison service were seen as no longer appropriate. In fact, no uniform was seen as appropriate. The uniform was out and grey lounge suits were in.

Rosters were drawn up and in order of seniority we all trooped off to the general stores to be measured by the ready-to-wear tailors. The weeks passed and eventually the great day arrived when we were all supplied with our issue of three suits each. A date was set for the change over and suddenly we had two hundred men arriving for work all wearing identical light grey suits, shirts and hospital ties. I wanted to cry out loud—*"a uniform is a uniform is a uniform"*—but who among the bureaucrats would listen.

Then the morning of the posting of results arrived. As there were only two students left, the paternal administration had given us the day off. The mail arrived very early but wasn't distributed to the staff pigeon holes in the staff block until about eleven o clock. We'd been informed to report to the chief male nurse at mid day. I hung around the corridor waiting. The other male finalist lived out and would know his results by now. No matter how often I looked at the hands on my watch they didn't seem to be going anywhere. Alf walked along the corridor with the mail and came across to me proffering a brown manila envelope. He gave me an encouraging smile.

"Here you are Gordon lad. Go and open it and then come down to the office and lets congratulate you."

I took the envelope.

"But what if I've failed." The butterflies in my stomach had turned into eagles and were hammering to get out. Alf smiled.

"Ah! Theel be reet."

I bolted up the stairs to the privacy of my room. Sitting on the edge of the bed I opened the envelope with trembling hands. The papers inside were folded in three. I started to unfold them and read. I didn't need any more than the first line. *"The registrar is pleased to inform you that...."* The eagles in my gut landed. I glowed as though a million little fires had started inside me. I had passed.

All that work was worth it. I was a staff nurse. I quickly read through the rest of the papers. Registration fees, uniform permit, certificate and badge. I was about to burst. I had to tell someone. I dashed down the corridor to find Frank and Dave. Dammit they were both on duty. Alf said come to the office. I ran down the stairs to the office, knocked on the door and almost ran inside.

"Told thee." Said Alf smiling. "Well done Gordon lad."

At twelve I saw the chief. Alf came with me and added his congratulations to the other student who'd also passed. The results were now posted on the hospital notice board and in the school. A quick telephone call home to tell the folks and then over to the school to thank big John and Mr. Sandy.

It was a great feeling seeing those other students still in the school and knowing they were a little envious of you because you'd already trod the road they were on. All four hospital candidates passed and that night saw a great celebration in the hospital staff club.

Even Alf and the other chiefs called in for a drink with us. We were, after all, trained like them. I think it was a great party. I don't remember too much about it and had to rely on Frank and Dave to get me to bed. I know it didn't cost me anything as everyone kept buying me drinks and wouldn't let any of the new graduates put their hands in their pockets.

The next few weeks were most enjoyable as I lived on a perpetual high. There is nothing like the boost to your confidence that the little piece of paper gives you. Then, imperceptibly, at first, I was dissatisfied. *Where do I go from here?. What is next?.*

Time was moving on and I had to think about further training or finding some new challenge. I couldn't see me at twenty one years of age being in Halley hospital for the rest of my life. I was still receiving a lot of satisfaction from the ward work, especially as I was always in charge when I was on duty and could implement some of the things we'd been taught in the school, even if only in a small way.

It was a time of re-appraisal and realisation began to dawn on me, as it did some of my peers. We were doing it all wrong. Well, not all of it, but too much wrong. How do we change this impersonal system? It will change—but very slowly. Maybe that is right. Slow change certainly won't disturb the security of the patients which is implicit in their routines. I couldn't wait. I had been at Halley hospital for nearly five years. It had made me grow up. Now I had to leave this sheltered and artificial environment and find a new world to conquer. Halley had changed for the better and part of me wanted to stay and continue to work for and with the change. Yet, I knew that if I stayed I'd contribute less than if I went away to grow some more. I could always come back.

My mind was made up. I noticed more and more general hospitals were accepting male students for nurse training and that post graduates got reasonable pay. Then there was that lovely general nurse student I once knew. There may be plenty more like that in the general hospital.

So that's it—goodbye Halley hospital—I'm off to do my general training perhaps I might even become a Miracle Worker.

And that is another story.

**If you liked Random Reflections of a Looney Bin then watch out for the sequel. Random Reflections of a General Hospital -Coming soon.
Now read on**

Postscript

This postscript is not part of Random Reflections but is a personal viewpoint of the author offered here as food for thought.

Today we seem to be far away from those early days in mental health and disability services. Since my time at Halley I have worked in a wide variety of health settings. In most countries the large institutions are a thing of the past. Parsimonious Governments and Health Services welcomed with open arms the message of community care implicit in the works of Bengt Nirge, the father of Normalisation, and later by Wolf Wolfensberger with his almost hysterical model of "Social Role Valorisation" with institutions portrayed as places of brutalization and death making.

Rightly, I believe, the model of deinstitutionalization became a goal and the institutions were closed and the inmates decanted into society in a wide range of accommodation options. But, in our haste to save money, did we forget that those people who are different, are not well tolerated in the community. Governments finds it easier to ignore individuals while large groups in institutions and their voting and organized parents do not go away easily.

Small groups homes sprang up in communities all round the world. Some work brilliantly and some function worse than the most despicable institution. Imagine being in a home of 5 or 6 unrelated people whom you don't know and don't want to know. The only visitors are the staff, who are paid to be there, or the people providing services like utilities. You are dependent on others for all your living needs and you don't go out unless the mini bus is available. You cannot walk your community as your are considered a risk to other people, or a risk to yourself if you have seizures, or just an object of pity or dread and so the staff protect you from that community reality.

Other people are fortunate enough to live in communities of mutual care and understanding like L'Arch Communities (see appendix 2). While others have the benefit of Service systems based on the "Recovery Model"

Key aspects of this model include two guiding principles 'recovery as an individual process' and 'collaboration and autonomy support' and four skills-based components; change enhancement; collaborative needs identification; collaborative goal striving and collaborative task striving and monitoring (Oades et al., 2005).

However, not all people get the support they need. The residents in the institution frequently had the support of a revolving door—sometimes called a safe place to fall. When communities failed them they could always return to the Institution (home) for a while. Shrinking funding and rising numbers in many areas have taken away the safe place to fall and too many people with mental disorders are left to struggle with limited support in communities that are too busy to care.

Halley hospital had 56 children on the children's ward. Most children were cared for in the community. Heaven help the Doctor, Psychiatrist, or psychologist who wanted to label a child with the name of a condition other than those with clear physiological signs and symptoms like Downs syndrome, epilepsy, cerebral palsy or intellectual disability. Children did not, in the world of Halley, have psychiatric disorders. Most aberrant behaviours were managed well by parents and schoolteachers who had 50 pupils in a class and had never heard of a teachers aide.

Today we have over 24 million children worldwide who are on the medication Ritalin or Dexamphetamine for Attention Deficit Hyperactive Disorder (ADHD) A group of drugs with quite severe side effects for a condition which was only invented in 1987.

So I ask myself the question. Have we lost our way somewhere and allowed the system to take over—looking for a "quick fix" in a drug bottle—and a process which strives to label all human behavior.

Real care and services do not depend on the location of the service but on attitude. Perhaps best exemplified in this true tale of two people.

James went to his care worker after a day at the beach.

"I'd like to go sailing" he said.

The care worker made a note of his request and later in the week paid a visit to the local sailing club.

"I look after this person who has a mental disorder," she told the club Commodore," and he has expressed a wish to go sailing."

"Oh, I'm sure that can be arranged," the Commodore replied.

"Bring him along to the club next Saturday and I'll take him out in my boat. In fact if you know of any other people like him bring them along too, we could probably manage 5 or 6 people.

So it came to pass on a bright sunny Saturday 5 people with varying disabilities presented at the yacht club with a couple of care workers. They were squeezed, cajoled and helped into life jackets and with bare feet and slacks rolled up or skirts tucked in knickers, decanted into the flotilla of small sailing boats for a trip round the bay. The sea was calm, the wind was light, and the sailing was a delight.

It was generally agreed that the trip was worthwhile. All the people, with the exception of the young man who was seasick had a wonderful time.

It was great for the members of the small boat club. Their sport was also capable of bringing joy to others.

"Lets do it again next year" was the excited response from the members and care workers alike.

An ad-hock committee was formed and before you know it the "Small boat clubs outing for the disabled" was born.

The first weekend after Easter each year small boat owners from all over the state converge on the beach. People with all types of disability converge on the beach in coaches (free of charge from rural areas) or free maxi taxis (no charge for the day) or with parents, care worker or friends. The local Rotary Club provide the refreshments and BBQ while the Lyons Club look after the drinks and other community groups provide wheelchair pushers and all manner of help. And so it continued for many years.

Contrast that event with this.

Bill went to his care worker after a day at the beach and said.

"I'd like to go sailing"

The care worker smiled and said

"I'll pick you up on Saturday morning."

Sure enough on Saturday the care worker picked Bill up and the drove to the local yacht club. They went in to the club house and the care worker signed them in as visitors. They sat at a table in the club, had a drink and watched the yachts sailing up and down the bay, occasionally venturing outside to watch the boats hauled up out of the surf. The morning passed quickly and after a snack lunch in the club house it was time to go home.

"Shall we come again next week?" asked the care worker.

Bill was only too pleased to come again and so the care worker picked him up as usual on the Saturday morning. The club was busy and as they sat at "their" table the club was filling up. There was a regatta on and the place was a hive of activity with lot to see and take interest in. The care worker answered Bills questions as best as she could and promised to find the answers to things she didn't know. As the morning wore on many of the people in the club house drifted outside to watch the races from the beach. The tables were full of empty glasses and beer bottles.

"Why don't you collect some of those empty bottles and glasses and take them back to the bar for the barman" suggested the care worker to Bill.

Always happy to oblige Bill busied himself taking the empties to the busy bar man and placing them on the end of the bar and was rewarded with a Coke for his trouble

This pattern continued for a couple more Saturdays and Bill continued to collect empties and was rewarded with a drink and thanks. The Care worker asked about non-sailing membership and filled in the application forms for them both to become members.

When the care worker was not available Bill walked to the club to collect the glasses. One particularly hot summer day the barman asked Bill to take a couple cans of beer to some men working on a small yacht by the clubhouse slipway. Some other men working, saw the cold beers and asked Bill to do the same for them. So another task was added to Bills visits to the club. He now collected empties and delivered drinks to men working on their boats.

One day a yachtsman, taking his beer from Bill said.

"Have you ever been out on a sail boat?"

"No" Bill replied.

"Would you like to?"

"Yes please" There was no escaping Bills enthusiasm. A few hand gestures to the care worker and Bill was in life vest and going for his first sail round the bay.

Six months later Bills membership was changed to sailing member and he was often looked for to help crew a boat when a team was one short for competition. He still ferried drinks and collected glasses for the bar and was missed if he was away. He had achieved his wish and "gone sailing."

As far as I know Bill is still a member of that yacht club today.

The interesting thing about these two stories is this. James lived at home and his care worker was the Disability Services Social worker. Bill lived in the large institution and his care worker was his mental health nurse.

Often the success of Mental Health Support is not where the person resides but the attitude and insight of those who care for the people with mental health problem, and often the attitude of the community.

One of my hero's John McKnight said at a conference many years ago.

"Systems will only serve Systems—It is in Communities that people will Grow and Live.

Appendix 1

"Rules of Halley Hospital—
certified institution for mental defectives."

1. The gatekeeper shall record the names of all persons who pass through the institution gates, in the book provided for the purpose, with the time at which they enter and leave.
2. No person whatever, except members or officials of the County Mental Hospitals Board, or the Board of Control, shall be allowed admission to the institution, except with the express permission of the Superintendent or the Clerk and Steward, unless the gatekeeper, by his own knowledge, or by that of some person on whom he can place reliance, knows that the person demanding admission has permission to visit.
3. Female patients shall, in all cases be attended by female nurses.
4. A male nurse shall not enter a division of the institution appropriated to females, except on duty, and then only if accompanied by a female nurses.
5. A female nurse shall not enter a division of the institution appropriated to males, except on duty, and then only if accompanied by a male Nurse
6. No nurse shall leave the ward except in cases of emergency, or in the discharge of an assigned duty, without the sanction of a medical officer, the Matron or Head Male Nurse.
7. Nurses must always retain their keys in their personal possession whilst on duty and must never, on any account, lend them to a patient. Institution keys must not be taken away from the institution except by nurses on duty unless with the permission of the Superintendent and such keys shall be deposited with the gatekeeper at the main lodge.

8. It is the duty of every nurse to treat patients with kindness and humanity, to listen patiently to, and to report their complaints and grievances, and at the same time to be firm in maintaining order and discipline, and repressing unduly loud talk and laughter in the wards and workrooms and enforcing complete observance of the regulations of the institution.
9. Nurses must at all times maintain a strict supervision to ensure that patients shall not run the risk or have the opportunity to cause injury to themselves.
10. Pokers and fire Irons must always be kept locked away except when in actual use, and patients must not be allowed to bring with them into the wards any tools or implements with which they might injure themselves or others.
11. The clothing of patients shall be searched at bedtime.
12. Nurses shall see that their patients are clean and tidy and ready to sit down to their meals punctually at the specified times.
13. The nurse in charge shall say grace before meals.
14. Patients are not allowed to change articles of food with each other, or remove food from the table, do needlework or indulge in loud talking.
15. The amount of food taken by epileptics should be particularly noticed and no epileptic may take a meal except under supervision.
16. After every meal, the cutlery shall be collected, cleaned, counted and locked up. If any article is missing the Matron or Head Male Nurse must at once be notified. In no circumstances must a patient be allowed the use of a carving knife or fork
17. Nurses are expected to present at all times when on duty a neat and tidy appearance.
18. Uniforms must always be worn on duty and only on duty.
19. No nurse, or other employee, may smoke whilst on duty.
20. A nurse, or other employee, may not introduce a pet or domestic animal, into the institution.
21. Nurses and other employees, resident in the institution will attend to the cleanliness of their rooms before commencing duty each day. They shall see that at all times during their absence from such rooms their personal property is secured under lock and key.

22. Fires are not allowed in nurses rooms except by special leave of the Superintendent. No fire must ever be left without being securely protected by a fire guard.
23. No employee resident in the institution many be absent from the institution after 11.20 P.M. Without the permission of the Matron, Head Male Nurse or housekeeper as the case may be.
24. No member of the staff shall, without the authority of the Superintendent bring or permit to be brought into any part of the institution any intoxicating liquor.
25. No member of staff shall, at any time or on any pretext, order or permit a patient to perform any work for the private benefit of a member of the staff or for the private benefit of any other person, without the permission of the superintendent
26. No member of the staff shall invite any person to visit the institution without the permission of the Superintendent and no member of the staff resident in the institution without like permission shall invite any visitor or guest to stay in the institution.
27. No member of staff or patient shall be allowed to enter the premises of the opposite sex without adequate authority. Any member of staff transgressing this rule, unless a satisfactory explanation be given to the Superintendent, shall be immediately suspended
28. There shall be as many nurses as shall be sufficient in the opinion of the Superintendent for the effective care of the patients by day and by night. No ward or house occupied by patients shall at any time be left without adequate staff.
29. Such patients as the Superintendent may permit shall at approved times and under such conditions as the Superintendent may direct, be allowed to take walks or to make excursions beyond the grounds of the institution.
30. A constant vigilance must be exercised by all members of the staff, particularly the nursing staff, to prevent escapes and all escapes shall be immediately reported to the Matron, Head Male Nurse and assistant medical officer.
31. The following precautions must be observed:-

Patients must be counted at meal times and at night.

Nurses shall, at frequent intervals, carefully examine all ward door locks, windows and window stops, noting particularly the putty around the glass of the windows and satisfying themselves that everything is secure. *(added after the great escape)*

32. When patients are exercising out of doors, proceeding to and from the various workshops and out in working parties, nurses and other employees shall so dispose themselves that every patient, so far as is possible, is under constant observation.
33. The senior nurse or other employee will see that this supervision is strict and that good order is maintained.

These rules were regularly observed and frequently broken at Halley Hospital during the time I was there. If you are entertaining the doubt that such a thing is not true or could not happen today. Take a look at the rules of any local institution. Church operated nursing homes are a good place to start. They do not have rules—they have policies which are exactly the same but with more words. One place I observed in 2003 in Queensland Australia had several hundred policies. All geared to keep the residents and the staff under control—and very little to do with care.

Appendix 2

L'Arche is an international federation of faith communities where people with and without an intellectual disability share life together. L'Arche, a French word for the Ark, seeks to create communities where people live a simple life of work, care, prayer and celebration.

L'Arche was founded in 1964 in a small French village by Jean Vanier who welcomed two men, Raphael Simi and Phillipe Seux, both of whom had an intellectual disability and were living nearby in a large institution. By living with Raphael and Phillipe, Jean discovered a way of the heart and a new way of living the beatitudes of Jesus.

From these simple beginnings L'Arche has grown into an international federation of 138 communities in over 30 countries.

In a world that is so divided and broken we want our communities to be a sign of reconciliation, hope and peace—a sign of God's love for us.

We are a very diverse group from all walks of life, some of our disabilities are obvious, some are hidden but all of us share in the mission of L'Arche, of changing the world one heart at a time.

Printed in Great Britain
by Amazon.co.uk, Ltd.,
Marston Gate.